Careful, Larson, don't let her beauty mess with your head.

How many times today had he admired her light bronze complexion, the sprinkling of freckles across her nose and those rich dark eyes? Not to mention the lush lips begging to be— He shook his head. *Think straight. She lives hand to mouth, picks up jobs here and there, doesn't stick with any particular thing for long. She's spent her life traveling the country, never settling down. She's just passing through.*

His fists opened and closed as he did battle with the two strongest organs in his body. His brain knew without a doubt she'd break Steven's heart. More than anything Kent wanted to protect his son, but he knew life had a way of playing out in the least expected ways. Why deprive the kid of the dazzling Ms. Desi?

Why deprive himself?

Dear Reader,

Welcome to Heartlandia, the little town with a big secret.

Sometimes a story comes to mind that challenges the heart and soul of the author. A biracial daughter of a Scandinavian mother and African-American father, Desdemona Rask grew up solely with her mother on the road in the Midwest. Deep in her heart Desi longs to find her family and her roots. After her mother dies she heads to her Scandinavian grandmother's house in the town from which her mother ran away. A whole new world opens up to Desi in Heartlandia, which is nestled along the Oregon coast by the Columbia River. There, a precocious eight-year-old named Steven becomes her first piano student. Next she meets his father, the striking doctor next door, and that's when the fireworks begin.

Being a single father of a super-active son, and running the local urgent care clinic, Kent Larson hardly has time to breathe, let alone fall in love. When the exotically lovely daughter of his childhood babysitter arrives in town, new life gets infused into Kent's heart. But how can he trust his heart again when his wife walked out on him and their son without so much as a glance over her shoulder? How wise is it to fall for a woman who has just set foot in town and is already searching for a way out through her family tree?

The heart is a funny organ that rarely listens to reason and logic. Thank goodness! Otherwise Desi and Kent would never have found their happily ever after.

I love to hear from readers. Friend me on Facebook or check out my website, www.lynnemarshall.com.

Wishing you love and happy reading!

Lynne

A Doctor for Keeps

Lynne Marshall

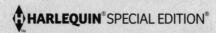

HARLEQUIN® SPECIAL EDITION®

ISBN-13: 978-0-373-65828-2

A DOCTOR FOR KEEPS

HARLEQUIN®
www.Harlequin.com

Printed in U.S.A.

Books by Lynne Marshall

Harlequin Special Edition

Courting His Favorite Nurse #2178
The Medic's Homecoming #2274
A Doctor for Keeps #2346

Harlequin Medical Romance

Her Baby's Secret Father
Her L.A. Knight
In His Angel's Arms
Single Dad, Nurse Bride
Pregnant Nurse, New-Found Family
Assignment: Baby
Temporary Doctor, Surprise Father
The Boss and Nurse Albright
The Heart Doctor and the Baby
The Christmas Baby Bump

Other titles by Lynne Marshall available in ebook format.

LYNNE MARSHALL

Lynne used to worry that she had a serious problem with daydreaming—then she discovered she was supposed to write those stories! A late bloomer, Lynne came to fiction writing after her children were nearly grown. Now she battles the empty nest by writing stories that always include a romance, sometimes medicine, a dose of mirth, or both, but always stories from her heart. She is a Southern California native, a dog lover, a cat admirer, a power walker and an avid reader.

Sincerest thanks to Tara Gavin for giving me the opportunity to write this book and series.

Special thanks to my friend Sylvie Fox for her input in a key scene.

As always, thanks to my steady-as-a-rock critique partner, Dee J. Adams.

Chapter One

Desi wished she had a flashlight as she crept around the side of the ancient house in the dark. A thorn from an equally old and gnarly bush snagged her T-shirt, puncturing her skin.

"Ouch!" She immediately regretted her outburst since it was almost midnight. *Where did Gerda say that painted rock is?*

Her grandmother, a woman Desi had met only a few times in her twenty-eight years, had earlier instructed over the phone where the extra house key was hidden. Determined not to wake up Grandma Gerda, she tramped through the overgrown grass and shrubbery along the side of the house, searching for the mark.

Success! A brightly patterned rock nestled against the wooden gate stood out under the moonlight like fluorescent paint under black light. As she'd been told, she searched along the bottom for the small stick-on box holding the house key, hoping there weren't any nighttime creepy crawlers around. Just as she retrieved the box and opened it, the assaulting aroma of night-blooming jasmine tickled her nose. Sneezing with gusto, she dropped the key and got on her hands and knees to search for it, grateful there was a full moon.

A few seconds later, with key in hand, she emerged out of the thick overgrowth between two houses, heading for the huge wraparound porch belonging to her maternal grandmother. But not before tripping on a brick along the walkway. She lurched forward, swatting at the night for nonexistent support and letting fly a few choice words.

A bright light blinded her just as she stopped teetering and regained her balance.

"Who's there?" A distinctly deep and masculine voice came from the vicinity of the light.

She shielded her eyes with her forearms. "I'm Mrs. Rask's granddaughter. Who're you?"

The light lowered, allowing Desi to see a huge shadow, making her wish she'd kept up those kickboxing classes… just in case.

"I'm Kent, Gerda's next-door neighbor." The man stepped closer, studying her, as though he didn't believe her story. "I've never heard about a granddaughter."

Why would she expect otherwise? Wasn't she supposed to be the secret granddaughter? Especially since a Scandinavian stronghold like Heartlandia along the Columbia River in Oregon probably wasn't used to people like her.

"Are you saying you're Ester's daughter?" His voice, a moment ago deep and intriguing, had jumped an oc-

tave higher. He must have known who her mother was…
or had been.

"Yes. Could you please turn off that light and not
talk so loud? I don't want to wake my grandmother. I
had no idea how long the drive from Portland to Heartlandia would be." On a whim, and for future reference,
she'd taken a detour through the big city just to see it,
suspecting her father might still live there. Determined
not to spend extra money for a motel, she'd made a decision to drive straight through tonight. "Took me two
and a half hours. And what's Oregon got against street-
lights, anyway?" she said in a raspy whisper. "Thought
I'd driven into a black hole on Highway 30 for a while
there." She fussed with the leaves that had stuck to her
shirt and her hair, and brushed off the dirt from her
hands, then reached out. "I'm Desi Rask, by the way."

Stepping closer, with her eyes having adjusted to the
dark again, she realized how tall the man was. At five
foot nine it was hard to find many men to look up to.
He had to be at least six foot three. And blond. As in
Nordic-god blond. "Kent Larson." He accepted her hand
and shook it; hers felt incredibly petite inside his grasp.
"Your mother used to babysit me before—"

He stopped without completing the sentence. *Before
she ran away from home.* Yeah, Desi knew the story.
Her mother, the piano-bar queen of the Midwest, had
finally cleared up most of the missing pieces before
she'd passed.

"Desdemona? Is that you?" a reedy voice called out.
"Kent?"

Succeeding at doing what she'd hoped to avoid—
waking up her grandmother—Desi turned toward the

porch to face her for the first time since her mother's last days in the hospital.

"It's me. Your greeting committee from next door decided to interrogate me before I could let myself in."

"That's not it," Kent the Viking said. "With Mrs. Rask being the mayor, I look out for her is all."

She'd seen the doubt on his face and the hesitation to swallow her story when she'd told him who she was. But being half-black, why should she expect otherwise when she didn't look anything like the Norseman or her equally pale grandmother, the mayor of Heartlandia?

Kent worked quickly to put two and two together. Ester Rask had been a teenager when she'd run away from home. Being only eight at the time, the same age as his son Steven now, he'd never heard the whole story. He remembered the town searching high and low for Ester without success. He also remembered that Ester had never been declared dead, just missing, and eventually, his parents had quit talking about her disappearance altogether and he'd had a new babysitter. That had to be twenty-eight years ago. Hard to believe.

Now, having run into Desdemona in the dark of night, he understood why Ester had run away—she must have been pregnant.

Gerda flipped on the porch light, and Kent got his first good look at the dark and enchanting one named Desdemona. Or Desi, as she'd introduced herself. Tall, sturdy in build, coffee-with-cream-colored skin with an extra dollop of milk, wide-set rich brown eyes, a smoothed out variation on the pointy Rask family nose, full lips and straight teeth. It had been a long time since he'd seen such an exotically beautiful woman in person and it threw him off-balance.

She wore a bright yellow top that hung off one shoulder, with the straps of a black tank top playing peekaboo from beneath. The midnight-blue jeans fit like second skin, and black flats countered her height. Wow, her outfit didn't leave a whole lot to the imagination, and right now his was running wild. Loads of thick dark hair danced around her shoulders, long and full-bodied like how he'd remembered Ester's, except Ester's hair had been blond, nearly white-blond. Kent's hands grew suddenly restless, his fingers itching and his mind wondering what it would be like to dig into those gorgeous waves and curls.

Even at eight he'd had a crush on his babysitter, and tonight a fresh rush of infatuation was springing up for another brand of Rask woman.

She'd introduced herself as Desi Rask, so Ester had probably never married. For some reason, maybe his general mood about marriage lately, that knowledge landed like a sad clunk in his chest.

"Are you going to come inside?" Mayor Rask asked, drawing him out of his rambling thoughts.

"Oh, no. Steven's sleeping. I should be getting back."

Desi didn't hug her grandmother when she approached the porch. Instead they stood with a good three feet between them, offering polite smiles, seeming more like mere acquaintances than relatives. It didn't feel right by a long shot, but who was he to figure out the way life should go?

"Let me get my stuff first," Desi said, rushing back down the six porch steps toward the Ford Taurus station wagon from at least two decades back. That car had definitely seen better days.

"I'll help you," he said on impulse, waiting for her to open the back liftgate. There were two suitcases, a few boxes and assorted household items, including a potted plant or two. Was she moving in?

"All I need is my overnight case for now."

Maybe she was just passing through.

"I can get whatever else I need in the morning," she said, her alto voice already beginning to grow on him. Would she still be there by the time he got off work tomorrow?

"May as well bring this one inside, too." Ignoring her wish, he grabbed both suitcases and carried them up the porch and inside his neighbor's house. This one gave the impression of being flighty, and he wanted to make sure for Gerda's sake that her long-lost granddaughter stuck around for more than one stinking night. Surreptitiously catching Gerda's gaze on his way inside the dimly lit house, he inquired with a raised brow, "Everything okay?"

She nodded in her usual stiff-upper-lip way, clutching the thick blue bathrobe to her throat. "She'll have Ester's old room, upstairs and down the hall." Gerda's robe was the exact shade of blue as Desi's painted-on jeans, and he wondered if either woman noticed their similar taste in color.

Kent carried the bags around the grand piano in the center of the living room—the piano he'd once taken lessons on and now Steven also took lessons on—and headed up the stairs. The third door on the left was the room where Ester had taught him how to play Go Fish. He knew this house like it was his own, having lived next door nearly his entire thirty-six years. Being so deeply rooted in Heartlandia when his parents moved to a retirement village in Bend, he'd bought their house.

As a doctor and part owner of the Heartlandia Urgent Care, he had an early shift tomorrow, so he excused himself. "Welcome to Heartlandia, Desdemona, but I've got to go."

Desi sent a hesitant but thoughtful glance his way just before he headed for the door, her eyes filled with questions and suspicion. He nodded good-night, recognizing the mistrustful look, since he saw the same expression each morning when he shaved. When had he lost his natural trust in women? Oh, right, when his wife walked out.

"Gerda, I'll check in tomorrow."

"Tell Steven to be sure and practice," Gerda said, reminding Kent that his son could come up with a hundred excuses when it came time to take his piano lesson.

A few minutes later, lying on his bed, hands behind his head on the pillow, Kent stared at the ceiling, wrenching his memory all the way back to when he'd been eight. Ester Rask had run away and had never come back. So much of the story had eluded him all these years. Now he understood it was because she was pregnant. He'd never known that part of the equation before. He'd heard she'd died last year, seen how distraught Gerda had been when she'd come home from her mysterious trip to California just before she'd been appointed mayor pro tem. Yet she'd barely spoken about it, just moped around for months. At least Gerda had been able to see her daughter one last time—a sad consolation to a lost life together.

Now, like a prodigal granddaughter, the woman named Desdemona had shown up.

The downright sadness of all the lost family years hit him where it hurt most—in the gaping wound his wife had ripped open when she'd left him. As he clearly didn't need to be reminded, Gerda wasn't the only one moping around for months on end.

He shook off the negative memories, choosing to focus on the stars outside his window instead of the ache in his heart.

The strangest thing of all was, tonight he'd immediately reacted to Desi's exotic beauty when he saw her under the soft glow of the porch lamp. But that was such a shallow response. He should ignore it. Yet, in the still of the night, under the gentle beams of moonlight, he couldn't get her or those questioning, mistrustful brown eyes out of his mind.

Tall and well proportioned, with extra-fine hips, she was a woman who'd fit with his big, overgrown frame. He grimaced. Why torture himself and think about women? After seven years of marriage, he couldn't make his wife stick around. Not even for Steven's sake. Why fall for their beauty when their motives cut like blades? He ground his teeth and rolled over, willing the young mysterious woman out of his thoughts and demanding his mind go blank so he could finally fall asleep.

The next morning, Desi threw on an old sweatshirt and baggy jeans and made her way down the creaky staircase of the ancient house. Gerda was already up and reading the newspaper, and jumped up from the table the moment Desi set foot inside the kitchen. They tipped their heads to each other in a silent greeting. Like strangers.

"I don't drink coffee, but I've got some if you'd like," Gerda said, sounding eager to please.

"Thanks, but if you show me where you keep it, I'll be glad to make it myself. Sit down."

The thin and almost ghost-white woman pointed to the cupboards near the back door before sitting again. "Your mother always loved coffee, even when she was young. I used to worry it would stunt her growth, and she was only five foot three when she left." Silence dropped like a forgotten net. But Gerda quickly recovered. "I know it's silly, but I've always kept her favorite brand on hand, even now when I know she'll never come—" The sentence broke in half as Gerda lost her voice.

Desi rushed to her grandmother and put her hands on those bony shoulders, her own throat thickening with loss and memories of a family she'd never gotten to know.

Gerda reached up and tentatively patted one of Desi's hands with icy-cold knobby fingers. "I'd asked your mother to come home so many times."

"I know you did. Mom finally told me." Mom had felt fragile like Gerda the last few months of her life. Desi could only imagine how hard it must have been for a mother to lose her daughter when they'd been estranged all those years. As for why her mother had never returned, well, that mystery wasn't likely to be resolved.

"Well, you don't have to worry about coffee stunting *my* growth," Desi said, deciding to change the subject. "I'm five foot nine."

Gerda offered a wan smile and Desi waited for her

face to brighten, even if only a little, then she went back to making the coffee. Gerda sipped hot tea and ate a piece of toast with marmalade, putting the taste for toast and jam in her mind. *Mom loved orange marmalade, too.*

Since Gerda seemed engrossed in the morning paper, and Desi wasn't sure what to talk about anyway, she filled her coffee cup and wandered into the living room, to the gorgeous grand piano in the center of the room. She took a sip of coffee and carefully placed the cup on an adjacent TV tray containing a bowl of candy and a pile of colorful stickers.

Lifting the keyboard cover, she explored the keys, enjoying the feel of the cool ivory beneath her fingers. She'd had to sell her mom's piano when she'd sold the house in L.A. to pay for the medical costs. She'd put the remaining contents of that house of memories into storage, the piano and everything it represented in their lives being the biggest memory of all. Music, and her mother's talent, had been their bread and butter, keeping them afloat through all the tough times. And there had been many.

When Desi became old enough to work and was able to contribute toward house payments, they'd finally settled into their own home. Though she'd never been sure where the large down payment had come from, Desi had a sneaking suspicion her grandmother had something to do with it. Then her mother got sick. All those years in smoke-filled lounges had finally caught up with her. Four years of lung-cancer treatment and suffering for naught. Even after Mom had died, Desi was hit with huge medical bills.

As she so often did when she felt sad or moody,

like right now, Desi turned to music. Soon her fingers danced along the keys, as if having memories in their tips. Beethoven's "Für Elise" filled the room with the rich tone of the grand piano. When she'd finished, she moved on to a Chopin nocturne. On and on she played, forgetting all her worries, losses and fears, until her fingers and hands were tired. She hadn't played perfectly, far from it, but what could she expect for not having touched a piano in months, since she'd sold theirs? Still, it felt good. Invigorating.

Desi sipped her tepid coffee then smiled, her mood elevated. She glanced up and found Gerda leaning against the kitchen door, tears brimming in her pale eyes.

"Your mother taught you well," Gerda said.

Desi nodded. "She did. She loved music. All kinds. But you probably knew that."

"I taught her how to play, you know." Gerda stood straighter. "She was such a natural."

The questions swimming in Desi's head almost poured out of her mouth: *Why did mom need to run away? Why did she rarely talk about you? Why did Mom insist it was just the two of us? What could have been so horrible for her mother to run away and sever all ties?* But seeing her grandmother's fragile state, the emotion she wore on the shabby midnight-blue bathrobe sleeve, Desi kept her questions silent.

"Do you still play?" Desi asked.

Gerda's eyes brightened, and she proudly walked toward the piano. "I'll have you know, besides being mayor pro tem of Heartlandia, I'm also the most sought-after piano teacher in town." A mischievous smile stretched her sallow and lined cheeks as she sat on the other half of the bench. "For anyone under the age of twelve, that is." That explained the candy and stickers.

Gerda chuckled and it sent a chill down Desi's center. Her mother had laughed exactly like that. Up close, though Gerda's eyes were milky blue, they were shaped like her mother's, and though Gerda's hair was all white now, she could tell that it used to be blond, also like her mother's. The two women fit together like misplaced puzzle pieces, and why wouldn't they, since they were mother and daughter?

Yet Mom had said very little about her family over the years. That was until her last days. All Desi knew growing up was the road and hotels and Mom. No strings. Just the two of them. Deep down Desi had always suspected it was because she was of mixed race that they'd kept to themselves. Though her mother had not once hinted at that being the reason. Being constantly on the road, with her mother working for a big Midwest hotel chain as the lounge entertainment, playing one month here, six weeks there, made it impossible to make friends or, evidently, keep in touch with relatives. Only on her mother's deathbed had she asked for Gerda to come. And Desi had finally learned about the man named Victor Brown, the father she never knew.

Gerda had started playing a song meant as a duet. Desi had been taught the same song by her mother when she was a kid. Without being asked, she jumped in and played her part in the higher octaves, and if that sparkle in Gerda's glance meant anything, Grandma was pleased.

They smiled tentatively at each other, then sat companionably for several minutes playing the piano together, and Desi was grateful that at least through music, they had a way to open up their communication. Otherwise, she felt like a stranger in a strange land in this place called Heartlandia.

"So you're the mayor?" she asked at the end of the piano piece.

Gerda nodded. "Not by my choice, but the town likes to choose its mayor from people long invested in Heartlandia." She looked straight ahead as she spoke. "I can trace my people almost back to the beginning. The only problem with that method is we get stuck in history, and these days we have a lot of new residents moving in because we have so much to offer families."

"Not keeping up with the times?"

Gerda glanced at her. "Something like that. I'm only temporary, though, and we'll have our general election next year. They promised the job wouldn't be hard, but I'm clearly in over my head."

"And then I show up."

Gerda hung her head. "Desdemona, I wish we could have one huge do-over where you are concerned. Your mother ran away because she was ashamed of being pregnant. We found her when you were born, and I am deeply sorry to say Edvard and I were surprised when we saw you. Ester was such a touchy one. Always had been. I didn't mean her to think what she did... You were my granddaughter. I loved you. But Edvard—"

"—couldn't accept that I was half-black?"

"It's not that simple, Desdemona. Please don't think that."

What was she supposed to think?

"I wanted to bring Ester and you home. She insisted she could take care of herself. I admit, I didn't fight hard enough and gave in to Edvard." Now Gerda connected head-on with Desi's eyes. "I kept watch over the two of you as best I could, though from a long distance. And I sent money whenever Ester was especially hard up."

Her mom must have kept those times to herself because in Desi's memory they lived hand to mouth most of their years on the road. But then, out of the blue five years ago when Ester first got sick, they were able to buy a small house. The home they'd always dreamed and talked about. The timing was perfect, since her mother couldn't keep up with traveling and chemo. Had her mom been saving Gerda's money, or had Gerda helped out, as she'd previously suspected?

There was a reprieve from the cancer and Ester was able to take a few playing jobs here and there, but the cancer came back. Even then, Ester stayed away from Heartlandia.

"Why didn't we ever visit?" Desi asked. It was an honest question that her mom had always evaded.

"It wasn't because I didn't invite you. Please know that. Your mother—" Gerda hung her head again. "She just didn't want anything more to do with her home, I guess."

Desi's heart tightened. It must have been hard for Gerda to be rejected time and again by her daughter. Deciding they'd shared enough heartache for one morning, she went back to playing another simple song and soon Gerda, accepting the quiet reprieve, joined her.

After a few more duets and small talk, they went their separate ways, Gerda to spend some time at city hall and Desi to shower and dress.

She did some laundry and took a walk around the backyard, trying to figure out why her mother had been so stubborn, insisting on keeping her to herself despite the invitations to come home.

An abundance of rosebushes in assorted colors filled the air with a strong fragrance. A huge white hibiscus bush in the far corner seemed no less than twelve feet high. The Victorian-style house hadn't looked nearly as bright yellow in the dark of night. Trimmed in green, with a pitched roof and a third-story dormer with a fan-light window, the house looked like something out of an old movie. Desi circled the perimeter of the house and noticed a partially covered balcony at the front and a second balcony on the side. What a gorgeous place… the home her mother had run away from.

Returning to the scene of the crime of last night—the gated side yard with overgrown bushes and shrubs— she glanced next door at another Victorian. It was painted completely white with a small bay window at the front, the only color in sight an aqua-blue door at the side entrance. Kent's house almost looked medicinal. Churchlike. She wandered toward his house, noticing the artful subtleties of the architecture. But white? Really? It seemed such a waste.

Soon growing bored with trying to figure out why the big guy had the blandest house on the block, Desi's gaze drifted to the imposing Columbia River several blocks away, down by the railroad tracks and the docks. The water twinkled beneath the strengthening sun. In the distance, the longest bridge she'd ever seen arched from this side of Oregon far across to what she assumed must be Washington State.

Though June, the brisk air brought gooseflesh to her arms even through her light sweater. She turned to go back inside. On the hillsides behind her stood dozens and dozens of more modest but brightly painted Victorians overlooking the jagged riverbank. Scattered among the Victorians were dwellings of half timber wood–half brick foundations with tall sloping roofs, reminding her of her Scandinavian heritage.

Her surname, Rask, was Danish, but according to her mother, she'd come from a place filled with Norwegians, Swedes, Finns and Icelanders along with the original Chinook peoples. When Ester rarely did talk about "home," to Desi's ears it sounded like a mythical place, perhaps a figment of her mother's dreams, someplace she embellished to feed the imagination of her young daughter. This vista seemed to prove the point. It did almost look mythical.

Her mother had run away from an idyllic, lost-in-time town called Heartlandia. Or Hjartalanda, as the welcome sign at the edge of town said. She'd scoffed when she'd read the slogan beneath: Find Your Home in Heartlandia.

Was it possible? Could a quaint town fill up that huge hole inside her?

She headed up the stairs to her room. Seeing her grandmother again was only half of the reason for this trip to Oregon. The other half was her father.

A couple of hours later, after doing research on her laptop, Desi's stomach growled. She wandered down to the kitchen, searching for food, but instead found Gerda home and fumbling with a rubber opener and a stubborn jar.

"Let me get that for you," she said.

With a look of defeat in her eyes, Gerda handed over the jar. "My arthritis is giving me fits today." She rubbed her hands and grimaced. "Guess I better start making phone calls and cancel tomorrow's piano lessons."

"How many students do you have lined up?"

"Four. I give lessons from two to six on Tuesdays and Thursdays since I do the part-time mayoral work on Mondays, Wednesdays and Fridays."

"All kids?"

Gerda nodded while searching the cupboard, looking at medicine bottles one by one until she found what she wanted.

"Any advanced students?"

"Oh, heavens, no. They're all beginners in book one or two." She shook out a couple of pills into the palm of her hand. "The next generation of great talent, as I tell their parents."

"Why don't you let me take over for you?"

"I couldn't ask you to do that," she said, filling a small glass with water and popping the pills into her mouth.

"I'm offering. It's the least I can do since you're letting me stay here as long as I want."

Gerda folded her arms, her eyes nearly twinkling. "That would be wonderful."

At five o'clock the next afternoon, a timid tap at the front door let Desi know the last student had shown up. Gerda had been so impressed with Desi's teaching style, she'd dropped out of sight after the beginning of the four-o'clock lesson. Desi suspected it was to take a nap, as she'd been yawning throughout most of the last lesson.

Desi opened the door and found a towheaded boy

with bright blue eyes, who was a little chunky around the middle. "Hi! Are you Steven?"

He nodded hesitantly. "Is Mrs. Rask here? It's time for my lesson." He waved three piano primer books like a fan.

"I'm substituting for Mrs. Rask today. She's my grandmother."

His eyes grew to the size of quarters. "You are? Wow. You don't look like her. You're pretty."

She laughed. The boy was already a charmer. Looked as though that Kent guy needed to take a few lessons from his son.

Last night Gerda had filled in Desi on all of the students. Steven was eight and showed potential, but he didn't put in enough effort to make much progress. Her job would be to light a fire in him for the joy of music. Tall order for a substitute.

The boy seemed tall for his age, and remembering his gigantic father, she understood why. Soon, when the growth spurts started, Steven would probably outgrow his chubbiness as she had when she was around that age.

Desi walked Steven to the piano, pulled out the bench and placed one candy where the boy could see it. "That's for after you show me your written theory homework."

He gulped. "Uh." He screwed up his face, making a bundle of tiny lines crisscross over his tiny nose. "I think I forgot to do it."

She bit back her smile, not wanting to let his cuteness get him off the hook. She subtly moved the candy back to the bowl and opened his book. "Well, then we'll work on it together, okay?"

The fill-in questions for note names and the staffs to practice making treble and bass clefs went by quickly with her guidance, and he brightened up. She put two shiny stickers on the pages, and he grinned.

Desi took the same piece of candy from the bowl and returned it to the prior spot. "Are you ready to play for me?"

He nodded, opened his book and dug right in. Clunky and uneven, he banged out the simple notes, but Desi could tell he'd put a lot of effort into his playing. Even to the point of grunting and muttering "uh-oh" or "dang it, I keep messing up."

She loved looking down at his silky white-blond hair and thought for a boy he smelled pretty good, too. Gerda had been right—Steven showed potential, but he just needed to be nudged. She patiently worked with him, curving his fingers just so, straightening his wrists and gently prodding his spine so he'd sit straighter. When he repeated his slouched posture over and over again, Desi realized he must have liked the way it felt when she walked her fingertips up his spine to get him to sit straight.

"That tickles," he said after the third reminder, smiling up at her, and her strict teacher persona melted around the edges.

When she explained some of the tricky parts of the song and showed him how to play it, she noticed his head had come to rest on her upper arm. The sweetie liked this attention. Maybe she could use that to make a piano player out of him.

"Would you like to learn a different kind of song?"

"Yeah, this one seems kinda dorky."

She played a simple basic blues song that used the bottom notes to make it sound snazzy. Steven sat right up, immediately interested in the piece. She found the page in the book so he could see the notes and showed him how to play the first few bars. He obviously liked the rhythm and soon his shoulders moved to the beat. She'd found it—his kind of song.

"I tell you what," she said. "You live next door, right?"

He nodded, making a serious face, exaggerating his already-deep dimples.

"If you want to come over here after school a couple days during the week, I'll let you practice on this piano, okay?"

"Will you be here?"

"Sure. I'll even help you practice if you want."

"Okay!"

The moment she'd finished carefully writing out his homework, the doorbell rang, and she jumped up to open it. The Norseman stood on the other side, overbearing in stature, first drilling a glance through her then peering inside the house. She'd forgotten how big Kent was. In daylight, his finely carved features and cutting blue eyes almost took her breath away. Too bad he chose to look so serious all the time. He wore a navy blue polo shirt, but the sleeves barely fit around his arms. The standard jeans fit very, very well, indeed.

She smiled a simple superficial greeting, while odd tingles threaded along her skin. "Come in," she said. "We just finished."

"Hi, Dad!"

"Hey, son."

Steven gathered his piano books and rushed toward his father. "Ms. Desi is a really cool teacher!" They hugged, and Desi could see the honest-to-goodness love they shared. It was the same kind of *you and me against the world* love that she and her mom used to have, and the display touched her deep inside. Maybe she'd cut the big guy some slack.

"That's great," he said to his son, then looked at Desi with near alarm in his glance. "Are you taking over for Mrs. Rask?"

"Just today. Her arthritis is flaring up."

"Won't you be my teacher next week?" Disappointment poured out of Steven's voice.

"We'll see how Gerda feels, okay?" She walked back to the piano and picked up the wrapped candy, then came back to Steven and handed it to him. "I promised to help you practice, remember?"

He took the treat as if he'd gotten the biggest present in the world. "Gee, thanks!" Throwing his arms around her hips, he hugged her and squeezed, his cheek flat against her stomach. Such a sweet boy. She couldn't say he was attention starved, not by the way his dad watched over him, but Steven sure liked being around her. It made her wonder where his mother was.

Midhug, she glanced up at Kent, her grin quickly shifting to a more serious expression. Though he tried to hide it, caution and warning flashed in his azure eyes, and the hair on the back of her neck alerted her to let go of Steven and back off.

She'd reacted instinctively to the boy and must have crossed over a deeply engraved line. She didn't have a clue why she'd tripped the alarm, but she'd respect Kent's nonverbal message. He watched steadily as she stepped away, and when they'd said their necessary goodbyes, all she could do was wonder what she'd done wrong.

Chapter Two

"Dad. Dad!" Steven pulled Kent's arm as he unlocked the front door, drawing him out of his thoughts. "Ms. Desi's the coolest piano teacher ever!"

"Mayor Rask is your piano teacher. Ms. Desi is just filling in." He wanted to set that straight, right off.

Steven charged for the electric keyboard in the corner of the dining room the second they'd hit the front door. As he turned it on, the excitement in his bright blue eyes was almost contagious. Kent held firm, refusing to get swept up in his son's enthusiasm. It wouldn't be a good idea to let Steven get attached to every woman who was kind to him. And that had been his pattern since his mother had left.

No one could fill the void his son must feel.

Steven had his music book opened and seemed raring to go before the keyboard was even warmed up. Transformed before Kent's eyes, the boy was the embodiment of eagerness—this from the kid who normally had to be dragged to piano lessons and who forced Kent's patience to get him to practice. Steven pounded out a simple song that had definite blues overtones, and it wasn't half-bad. The infectious smile on his face forced Kent to grin as he leaned against the wall, arms folded, listening. He loved seeing his son happy, especially after the rough couple of years they'd been through.

Blast it. The last thing he needed was for his son to have a crush on his substitute piano teacher—the woman who showed up in the dead of night and who might take off the same way. He couldn't bear to see any more disappointment in Steven's eyes.

How in hell was a child supposed to get over the heartbreak of his mother walking out at such a tender age, with not so much as a phone call on his eighth birthday?

If Kent had his way, Steven would have a couple of siblings by now, but that was the last thing Diana had wanted. Born and raised in Heartlandia, just like him, she wanted to move to a big city where she could spread her cosmopolitan wings and play wife to a doctor who made a staggering salary. She wanted parties and designer shopping sprees. She did not want to be married to a guy running his own urgent-care facility and having to be both businessman and doctor rolled into one. A guy who couldn't predict which side of the red line they'd land on at the end of each month.

She'd thought being married to a doctor meant she'd be home free, rolling in dough. What with staff salaries to pay, the never-ending need for supplies or new equipment, liability insurance up to his ears and the lease on that overgrown building, some months he had to take

a rain check on his own salary. Good thing he lived in
the same house he grew up in, the one his parents practically gave away when they sold it to him and moved
to Bend, Oregon, to enjoy their retirement.

Bottom line, Diana had wanted out. She'd wanted
to be far away. She'd wanted San Francisco, not Heartlandia. She'd wanted to be single again. Single without
a child hampering her whims.

"See, Dad? I can almost play all the notes."

"That's great." He applauded. "If you practice every
day, maybe you'll have it memorized by next week."

"Yeah! That would be the coolest. I could surprise
her."

"Now don't go getting ahead of yourself. She's only
substituting for Mayor Rask. She may not even be here
next week." Kent went into the kitchen to throw some
food together for dinner. Steven tagged along, practically on his heels.

"Can we invite Ms. Desi to the festival this weekend, huh?"

Kent didn't want to speak for someone else, but he
was quite sure Desi would be bored senseless at their
hokey small-town Scandinavian festival. Wasn't that
what Diana used to call it? "I don't know."

"I could buy her some *aebleskiver* with my allowance. I just know she'd love them."

Kent wanted to wrap his arms around the boy and
hold him close, tell him to be careful about getting his
hopes up where women were concerned. Instead, he
pulled open the cupboard and rustled around the canned
foods for some baked beans. He hoped to change the
subject with food, one of Steven's favorite topics. He'd
grill some chicken and steam some broccoli, and pre-

tend he didn't hear Steven tell him "for the gazillion-millionth time" that he hated broccoli.

"Dad? Dad! Can we?"

Kent quit opening the can, inhaled and closed his eyes. "We'll see."

"Please, please, please?"

"I'll think about it. Okay?" Feeling a major cave coming on, Kent went the diversion route. "Now go wash your hands."

Already having his father pegged, Steven triumphantly pumped the air with his fist. "Yes!"

The never-say-die kid sure knew how to work his old man. Kent quietly smiled and went back to cooking.

After dinner and a lopsided conversation with Steven talking about life on the school playground and one quick confession that he thought Ms. Desi smelled like his favorite candy—tropical-flavored SweeTarts—Kent mentally relented. Why allow his lousy attitude about women to get in the way of his son enjoying himself? Besides, when Kent was a kid he had a new crush every week. Steven would soon forget "Ms. Desi" and all would be back to normal.

After he cleaned up the kitchen he'd take a walk next door and ask Desi if she'd like to come along on Saturday. He wouldn't say a word to Steven, though, so the kid wouldn't feel the sting if she said thanks but no.

An hour later, Steven was showered and in his pajamas and planted in front of the TV in the family room.

Kent stared at himself in the bathroom mirror, wondering why in hell he felt compelled to brush his teeth and gargle before heading next door. He cursed under his breath as he headed downstairs toward the door. If he didn't watch it, next he'd be picking posies from the yard for the substitute teacher.

Nothing made sense about asking the new lady in town along just because his son wanted her to come. One thing was painfully clear, though. He'd been hanging out with eight-year-old boys too much lately. Then one last thought wafted up as he crossed his lawn, heading for Gerda's place—even an eight-year-old could see Desi was easy on the eyes.

Desi sat on a wicker glider on the large front porch behind the second arch, the huge living room window behind her. She'd thrown one of Gerda's warm shawls over her shoulders to ward off the chill from the night air. Under the dim porch light she was barely able to make out the print in the *Music Today* magazine she'd surprisingly found on her grandmother's coffee table.

Soon she'd have to switch to her eReader and that novel she'd started before she'd left home if she wanted to stay outside. And she did want to stay outdoors to give herself and Gerda some space. There'd been too many extended silences, too many bitten back questions from Desi and started but abruptly ended sentences from Gerda. So much to ask. So much to say. So hard to begin.

Tonight her grandmother seemed preoccupied with mayoral work, and Desi felt out of place. She stared at her scuffed brown boots, wishing she knew how to broach the subject of her mother. What was she like as a kid? Did she always love chili cheeseburgers? What made her think she had to run away when she got pregnant instead of telling her parents and working things out? But people were tricky. You couldn't always get right to the heart of the matter without first building trust, and her grandmother was obviously holding back the details.

She looked around the large, homey porch and inhaled the night air, even detected a hint of that jasmine from the side of the house. She twitched her nose. Something about this old house calmed her down, as if it had reached inside and said, *Hey, you might just belong here. This is where your mother grew up; these rooms, scents, colors, textures and sounds are your roots.*

Soles scuffing up the walkway averted her attention from her thoughts. Her gaze darted to the tall blond man from the bland house next door—the overprotective father with some sort of grudge—Kent.

An unnatural expression smacking of chagrin eclipsed his handsome face. It lowered his brows and projected caution from those heavy-lidded eyes. The sight of him set off a pop of tension in her palms.

He cleared his throat, and she closed the magazine. "Nice night, huh?"

One corner of her mouth twitched with amusement over his awkward opening. "Seems kind of cold to me."

"That's Oregon for you."

She smiled, deciding to toss the poor man a lifeline. "Is it?" When was the last time he'd talked socially with a woman?

"Yup. Unpredictable, except for rain." He came closer to the porch but not all the way up, one foot two steps higher than the other. He put his palms on his knee and leaned on them, an earnest expression humbling his drop-dead looks. "Listen, I want to apologize in case I came off cranky this afternoon."

She sputtered a laugh. "Cranky? My grandmother

might get cranky, but you, well, you seemed bothered. Yeah, that's the word—*bothered*."

He scratched one of those lowered brows. "Sorry."

"I was just being nice to your son, not planning on snatching him. Making him feel good about his progress, that's all."

"Yeah, and he couldn't stop talking about what a great teacher you are when we got home, too."

She smiled and magnanimously nodded her head. *Yes, I am a good piano teacher, thank you very much.* "Is that a bad thing?"

"Not hardly."

As he got closer, the tension in her palms spread to her shoulders, and she needed to stretch. Couldn't help it.

He watched with interest. "So anyway," he said, "this time every June we have this thing called the Summer Solstice Scandinavian Festival. Maybe your grandmother already told you about it?"

She shook her head.

"But as mayor pro tem she starts off the parade," he said.

"She hasn't said a word about it to me."

Gerda hadn't been feeling well tonight, and she'd seemed distracted after a hushed phone conversation. During dinner, Desi had talked about the piano students, even though a big question loomed in her mind. *Why couldn't you and Mom ever patch things up?*

"Really?" He seemed surprised.

During dinner, Desi couldn't bring herself to broach the subject about how bad their mother-daughter relationship must have been. Still, every indication—from the way her grandmother had opened the home to her to the way Desi caught her sneaking loving looks at her—suggested she was wanted. Yet that feeling of not belonging prevailed, along with the thought that Gerda was simply doing her duty out of guilt.

She shook her head at Kent. "The subject of an annual festival never came up."

"Well, the thing is, Steven would really like you to go with us to the parade and festival on Saturday."

Desi liked seeing the big man so completely out of his comfort zone and sat straighter. "So he sent you over to ask me out?"

Finally, a smile. Well, half of a smile. "Not exactly."

"He doesn't know you're asking, and you'd rather die than ask a tall, dark stranger to come along, so you snuck over behind his back to ask me to say no?"

The look he shot her seemed to ask, *Are you a mind reader?* Or she could be reading into it, just a wee bit.

"Not it at all. And, man, you've got quite an imagination." So much for her theory. He shook his head with slow intent. "I was thinking more that you'd rather pull weeds than be stuck with me for an afternoon. But Steven… He's a kick. He wants to spend his allowance on you."

She tilted her head, charmed by her young absentee suitor. "Not every day a male wants to spend his allowance on me. How can I refuse?"

Kent scratched the corner of his mouth. "You were right—I didn't tell him I was asking you in case you didn't want to come with us."

"How thoughtful of you, protecting Steven." Maybe he wasn't as bad as the vibes he gave off. "And thanks for giving me an out…but I'd like to go." *Sorry to disappoint.*

Surprise opened his eyes wide. His *sexy bedroom*

eyes—there were no other words for them. The sight of them did something deep in her belly, making her sit up and take notice. "I'm starting to feel a little cooped up in this big old house already, and I'd like to see the rest of the town." *See what my mother ran away from.*

His quick smile died before it reached his cheeks. "Before you take off again?"

"That's not what I meant." She didn't have time to analyze what stick had been surgically implanted into Kent Larson's spine, or why he was giving her such a hard time about coming and going as she pleased, so she ignored him. She'd stay in Heartlandia as long as she wanted or needed, and she didn't need his permission to leave when she was ready. "I meant, I'm looking forward to spending more time with Steven and seeing more of Heartlandia. And you can tell him I said yes."

"Good. That's good." He sounded hesitant. "Steven will be excited."

And what about you? She'd been around the country a few dozen times, but she wasn't bold enough to ask. Was her crazy physical reaction every time he came around by any chance mutual?

Did this Viking from the bland house next door have any soul? Any passion? He seemed to be bound by courtesy and what was expected of him. She couldn't put her finger on it, but something must have happened to make those invisible walls so high. Yet Steven was as lovable and huggable as a soft teddy bear.

At least Kent hadn't spoiled the boy with his stand-offish attitude. Yet.

With his mission accomplished, and without further words, Kent had already turned to leave.

"Tell Steven I'm really looking forward to going, okay?"

He tossed a thoughtful gaze back at her, took her in with a leisurely tour of her entire body. It was the first sign of life she'd seen in him since the night they'd met in the dark, giving her the inkling that maybe her physical response to him was reciprocated.

A subtle shiver rolled through her, and she clutched the shawl tighter and closer to her neck.

"I'll do that," he said. "We'll pick you up on Saturday morning around ten." And off he went, almost smiling, down the steps and toward the dark path home.

"Got it," she said softly, grateful the boy would be along to ward off the unexplainable reaction she had to the big guy with the aloof attitude.

Saturday morning was cool and damp, and Desi pulled her hair tightly back into a bun and covered it with a knit cap, careful not to catch her huge hoop earrings. She zipped her thin hoodie to the neck and did the final *is my butt too big in these jeans?* check via the full-length mirror. The doorbell rang and she stopped obsessing over what nature had given her and hustled out the bedroom door.

Gerda had answered the door already, and Steven and Kent hung back just outside on the porch, talking quietly.

"Oh, good, you're ready," Gerda said when Desi appeared at the top of the stairs. "I've got to go. Need to be there a half hour before the parade starts."

Desi rushed down the steps. "Don't let me hold you up."

Gerda was already on the porch and halfway toward her car in the driveway. "See you there!"

"We'll be by your booth for some *aebleskiver* later," Kent said.

Gerda's smile widened, setting off a network of wrinkles. "I'll make some fresh just for you," she said, looking at Steven.

She'd be manning the Daughters of Denmark bakery booth all afternoon after playing grand marshal. Somehow the old woman had become a figurehead for Heartlandia, and it was another duty she'd hesitantly accepted.

Pride broke into Desi's chest and she waved to her grandmother. "I'll be cheering for you!"

The car door closed and Gerda continued to smile as she backed out. It always caught Desi off guard how much of her mother she saw in her grandmother's face. So far they hadn't talked nearly enough about her mother, maybe because it was still too painful, but little by little they'd begun to forge their own cautious relationship.

After Gerda had gone, Desi looked at Kent. "Do I need an umbrella?"

"I've got it covered," Kent said, obviously enjoying his first glance at Desi, shaking her up with his sharp blue eyes. "You look like a Scandinavian flag."

Stopped in her tracks, Desi did a mental inventory of her choice of colors. A bright blue knit cap and red sweatshirt. "Gee, thanks. Just what every girl longs to hear."

"You look cool, Ms. Desi," Steven said, beaming at her.

Maybe she'd ignore the father and hang out with the son all morning. "Thanks, Steven." She stopped herself from messing his shaggy, nearly white-blond hair, knowing he wouldn't appreciate it—especially if he was planning to spend his allowance on her. And she had every intention of paying him back with the money she earned from her part-time calligraphy jobs.

"We better get going." Kent nudged Steven along with a hand to his neck. Steven halfheartedly tried to kick his dad's leg. Kent played along, kicking back, missing by a mile. The boy giggled.

Feeling a bit like a third wheel, Desi followed them off the porch toward the curb.

They rode over in a white—why was she not surprised—pickup truck, sitting three across with Steven between them. After a brief silence, Steven spoke up.

"The sons and daughters of Heartlandia first came together to start this festival fifty years ago," Steven recited like a tour guide for the city. "The early summer festival celebrates our Norwegian, Icelandic, Finnish, Swedish and Danish heritage—" he stumbled over some of the words, but managed to spit them out pretty well for an eight-year-old "—from the early fishermen settlers first stranded on our coast." He stopped long enough to swallow. "Our first peoples, the Chinook, saved and nursed our shipwrecked forefathers to health and taught them the secrets of hunting and fishing the waters of the great Columbia River." A quick picture of Linus explaining the meaning of Christmas to Charlie Brown came to mind with the quiet yet capable way Steven told his city's history.

"Okay, Steven, you don't need to repeat your entire class presentation for Ms. Desi."

"I liked it. Thank you, Steven."

"As you can tell," Kent interjected, "Hjartalanda is proud of both the Scandinavian and Chinook heritage."

"We have a special celebration for the Chinook peoples in—" Steven screwed up his face, eyes up and to the right. "What's that month, Dad?"

"October."

"Yeah, October. Then we have a beer barn, too, so that gets the old farts to come."

Desi sputtered a laugh before she could stop herself.

"Watch the language," Kent warned benevolently. "And, Steven, that's not *exactly* why we have the beer barn. It's—"

"That's what you said to Officer Gunnar that time."

Kent flashed a sparkling look at Desi over Steven's head. He enjoyed his son as much as she did. She lifted her brows. *You get yourself out of this one.*

"That was just an observation between him and me, and for your information, I said 'geezers,' not 'farts.'"

Steven giggled. "*Fart* is a funny word. I like it better. Fart, fart, fart." He dissolved into a fit of giggles.

"That's enough of that." Kent tried to sound stern, but the twitch at the corner of his mouth told a different tale.

Desi grinned at the father and son's candid conversation during the drive over. Maybe, if she kept quiet, she'd learn a heck of a lot more about Heartlandia—or Hjartalanda, as Kent had called it—than she'd found out from her grandmother so far.

Steven taught her a hand game for the rest of the short drive over, where one person would place their palms on top of the other, and the bottom person had to try to slap the upper person's hands. Something about his earnest approach to everything he did made her warm inside. He was easy to giggle, too, and she joined right in, even as she nearly got slapped silly from his quick reflexes.

They parked outside the central section of town and hiked up toward the main street called Heritage. Desi glanced far off at one end to see what looked like an official building, maybe city hall, with a totem-pole-type monument in front. She turned and gazed down to the other end, noticing storefronts, restaurants and other businesses in what seemed like a time warp to the 1950s architecture and style with evidence of 1970s expansion. One large building, six stories high, sat apart from the other mostly single- or two-story frames. It smacked of the Art Deco era of the twenties and thirties with geometric domes and lavish ornamental copper accents, which had turned green. Desi wondered if there was an ordinance about not building tall after The Heritage Hotel and Performance Center went up.

She'd slowed her pace to take it all in, and Steven grabbed her hand, pulling her along. Clusters of people grouped around the street corners and more lined the curbs with chairs and blankets to sit on. It seemed as if every person in the city had shown up for the parade.

"Move back, folks. Make way for the parade." A sturdy, broad-shouldered police officer spoke to the thickening group on one particular corner. The guy was built as if he could make a living on the side as a cage fighter.

"Quit harassing the locals. Cut us some slack, Sergeant, would you?" Kent's outburst made Desi tense. This wasn't the kind of guy anyone in their right mind should want to challenge.

The intense-eyed, equally handsome and obviously Scandinavian male turned to Kent. The grim expression on his face broke apart into a wide grin. "You give me a hard time and I'll haul your—" he glanced at Steven then back to Kent "—backside in."

The men shook hands, and Desi knew immediately they were friends. Respect shone through Kent's and the officer's eyes, and something else, too—something that looked a lot like brotherly love.

The policeman with light brown hair and flashing green eyes bent to greet Steven. "How'd you talk your old man into bringing you to the parade this year?"

"I asked my piano teacher along," Steven said, pointing to Desi.

Feeling suddenly on display, she made a closed-lip smile, stuffing her hands into the back pockets of her jeans. The officer looked her way and tipped his head, obvious interest in his gaze. She gave a single nod back.

"This is Mayor Rask's granddaughter, Desdemona," Kent said, reaching for her arm and encouraging her forward. "And this is Gunnar Norling, my best friend since grammar school."

"Hey. Nice to meet you," he said, casting a quick sideways glance at Kent, ensuring he'd get the lowdown later, before smiling at her.

"Call me Desi."

"Okay." He reached for her hand.

A drum-and-bugle corps rent the air, alerting the crowd the parade was about to begin, and Gunnar's attention immediately went elsewhere.

"Enjoy the parade, guys. I'm on duty." Off he went, looking attractive and official in the dark blue uniform.

The next thing Desi saw was the flag corps consisting of six teenage boys proudly displaying the five Scandinavian banners plus the U.S. pennant in the center. Each young man wore a vest in the traditional color of their country as they walked to the rhythm of three snare drummers directly behind them. Then came her grandmother sitting in the cab of an open horse-drawn carriage, waving demurely as she progressed down the street.

Desi waved wildly along with Steven and Kent, and Gerda's eyes brightened, stretching her Mona Lisa smile into a toothy grin.

As the procession continued, individual countries paraded their famous costumes and music while walking beside simple floats and automobiles.

The women and girls wore ankle-length dresses covered with colorful aprons and shawls or capes. Some wore white scarves on their heads, which made them look like flashy nuns, or little hats trimmed in red or blue. All the women wore thick stockings and what looked like homemade leather shoes. Large beaded necklaces seemed to be in vogue with many of the women in costume.

The men's outfits reminded Desi of a famous TV commercial for cough drops. She especially liked the bright vests and little turbans or knit caps with tassels some of the men wore.

The intense colors on all of the apparel impressed Desi—mostly reds and blues with some yellow—along with the pride and joy that poured out of every participant as they strolled by. She glanced at Steven and Kent and saw the same pride and joy on their faces.

"That's Viking," Kent said, pointing to one group.

Steven saw one of his friends walking with the adults and gave a holler. Kent grabbed him and gave him a noogie as they watched the group pass. The father and son touched affectionately a lot, she realized, and seemed to get along great. Mother or not.

"That's Swedish, my people," Kent said, as the next float approached.

The subtle differences between the groups were hard for her to see, yet everyone else seemed to know exactly who was who. What must it be like to belong so deeply to something, to have a heritage you could trace back thousands of years and know like the back of your hand? "Here come the Danes." Kent smiled and glanced at her. In the front row of participants was a young girl of mixed race, like herself, and she led the way. What was he trying to communicate, that she wasn't the only biracial person in town?

Heck, half of her family tree was cut off at the very first fork, a blunt and wide cut that ended with a single name—Victor Brown.

"Here come the Fins." Kent continued his parade coverage, his hands on Steven's shoulders and the boy's head resting against him, just above his belt.

Desi couldn't tear her attention away from the genealogy marching before her. She was made up of just as much of this as the other mysterious side, and today she deeply felt the Scandinavian connection.

"Here's my favorite, the Icelanders!" Steven jumped in, pointing ahead. "They always wear the funnest hats."

Besides the um-pa-pa sounds coming from some of the floats, there were others with fiddles that sounded so similar to what Desi knew as Celtic tunes. There was maypole-type dancing between some floats and livelier, showier footwork, knee and shoe slapping, among the boys and men between other floats. Her cheeks soon grew tired from all of the grinning.

As the parade went on, more modern versions of Scandinavian clothing came through. The easily spotted knit sweaters and caps, and stylish sheep-fur-lined boots sported by preschoolers and kindergartners grabbed her attention. A group of teens showed off what could only be described as *Scandinavian grunge,* complete with famous storybook red braids and raccoon-styled makeup, while doing gymnastics and a little street dancing.

Something was brewing and bubbling in Desi's chest. Could she see herself in the light faces of these people? Her mother's Nordic beauty was hard to detect when Desi looked in the mirror, yet it was there—her high cheekbones, the shape of her brows, the expressive eyes. Her mother was inside her—in every cell and in half of her DNA.

Her mother had run away and given up her entire life for Desi. She owed it to her to keep her mind and heart open to this town and all that it was and could offer. She needed to stick around long enough to learn who she was before she took off searching for the other half.

An hour after it had started, the parade came to a close with a final um-pa-pa group, and a small, sweaty hand on hers brought her back to the moment.

"Let's get over to the booths before the lines get too long," Steven said, tugging her down the street. So far the weather had cooperated, the earlier gray clouds parting, revealing bright blue sky above.

Kent walked a few feet away from them like a tall, benevolent chaperone giving them space.

"Is this where everything happens in town?" she asked over her shoulder.

"Pretty much. We've got a lot of touristy shops for the cruise-line visitors down toward the docks, but most of the travelers like to come up here to eat. We've got some great restaurants."

One redbrick restaurant and bar had a few tables out front and a black-and-white canopy under which an older African-American man sat drinking coffee as they passed. He wore a starched white chef's shirt and hat placed at a jaunty angle on his head. Their eyes met, as two standouts might, and he tipped his head at her without a hint of a smile. She smiled and repeated the gesture, noticing the name of the restaurant and promising to find her way back at some point. Lincoln's Place. "Good food since 1984. Live music and Happy Hour specials daily at the bar," the sign said.

Kent waved and the man lifted his palm in return.

Down the street was a small white restaurant, with a blue-and-yellow canopy out front, called Husmanskost.

"What's that?"

"They specialize in Swedish cuisine. I'll bring you some samples from the booths."

Desi kept walking, but her gaze stayed on the cute little restaurant, wondering what unusual tastes and dishes she'd find inside.

At the food section, the wait at Gerda's Danish Bakery booth was nominal. Gerda was already there working, and she smiled her greeting, then turned and picked up some already-packaged treats.

"I thought you were going to make the *aebleskiver* fresh for us," Kent said with a teasing tone.

"Even an old coot like me knows how to read phone messages. Steven texted you were on your way over as soon as the parade ended."

Desi shook her head and smiled over Steven's resourcefulness. Behind the counter on another surface were several grills with small round grooves filled with pancakelike batter. The other cook on hand used a toothpick to move the pastry ball around to cook it on all sides. It looked like a tedious job, and Desi knew she'd wind up with burned pastry if she were in charge.

"I gave you a mixture, Steven," her grandmother said. "Some have apples inside, others raspberry. Be sure to put extra powdered sugar on them. Oh, and I gave you different sauces to dip them in."

The fresh apple and cinnamon aroma of the small doughnut-hole-type baked goods made Desi's mouth water. "I'd like to try one with just the powdered sugar, if you don't mind."

Steven's face lit up. "That's my favorite, too!"

When they perched at a small table, Steven opened the box. Kent made a quick, stealthy reach right after Steven powdered them and popped one into his mouth.

"Hey, buy your own, Dad. These are for me and Ms. Desi."

Kent's brows shot up and, combined with the cheeks full of bakery goods, the vision made Desi laugh. He shrugged and said something completely unintelligible through his full mouth. A crazy urge to lick away some of the powdered sugar from his lips and chin gave Desi pause. What the heck was going on?

Of course she understood that Kent was an amazingly attractive man. It was apparent most of the women in Heartlandia—at least those at the parade who made obvious eyes at him—thought so, too. Besides, she was a healthy young woman who hadn't had a date in a long time. Of course she'd notice a guy like Kent. But this slow-heat in her lower parts whenever he was around still took her by surprise.

Step away from the merchandise. The last thing she needed was to complicate her circumstances by developing a crush on her grandmother's neighbor.

Kent slipped away as she and Steven gobbled down the delights. After they knocked off what was left of the dozen, grinning and smacking their lips all the way, Kent reappeared with a couple of containers. "Here you go."

"What's this?"

"I brought you some fish balls."

She didn't think she could eat another bite.

"Just a taste. Come on."

He fed her a nibble of the fish ball, and even though it was a stinky fish ball, all the while she thought this encounter was too intimate for a public place. "Mmm, that's delish."

"There's plenty more you'll have to sample." She glanced at his mouth and thought she'd like to sample that, too. "You haven't lived until you've had a midnight supper."

That sent her mind to a completely inappropriate place and her cheeks heated up. "I need something to drink."

"Steven, get Desdemona some water, will you, please?"

Her name seemed to simmer on his lips. Sheesh, he'd better make that ice water. "Thanks."

"If you'd like, I'll take you for a proper Swedish dinner sometime."

"Thanks, but I'm sure you're too busy with your clinic and all to do that."

"You know about the Urgent Care?"

"My grandmother couldn't be prouder of you if you were her own son."

"Did someone say my name?"

As more helpers arrived, Gerda had taken a break from her booth, coming around the corner and taking Desi by the elbow. "Steven, Kent, may I borrow Desi for a few minutes?"

Kent's police-sergeant friend showed up with a coffee in one hand and a huge Danish in the other. After delivering the water, Steven had waved to a few of the local boys, yet he still looked disappointed at the prospect of Desi leaving.

"I'll be back in a few minutes, okay?"

"We're going to do some boring booth shopping," Gerda added. "But you're welcome to come along."

Steven wrinkled his nose. "I'm gonna go play with my friends." He pointed to the group of boys chasing each other around for no apparent reason.

Kent waved his acknowledgment of everyone's whereabouts without missing a beat of the friendly conversation with his best buddy. Those guys seemed to really enjoy each other.

Traveling all her life had meant good friendships were hard to make, and that had always bothered Desi. What would it be like to have a special friend to share all of your thoughts with? Anytime she'd started to get to know a kid her own age, her mother would get a new hotel assignment in another city. Heck, Desi had always felt more like a mascot to the hotel housekeeping staff around the country than a friend to anyone.

Gerda guided Desi by several booths, making a stop in front of each one and introducing her. "Hey, everyone, this is my granddaughter, Desdemona." She couldn't seem prouder, and it gave Desi pause. If her mother had only given things a chance...

At the jewelry booths, she saw beautiful examples of the necklaces many of the parade participants wore and also brooches. Her eyes lit up at the meticulously knitted sweaters and hats at another booth two doors down.

"Oh, I love that red-and-white one," she blurted out.

"Try it on. Let me buy it for you," Gerda said.

"I can't let you do that."

"I've missed a lot of birthdays and Christmases. Please let me buy you a gift."

Feelings she wasn't prepared for folded into her heart. She reached out and for the first time hugged her grandmother. "Thank you."

"We'll take this," Gerda said midhug to the little lady behind the counter.

As they pulled back, Desi offered a sympathetic smile tinged with long-lost family ties. The tears in her own eyes were reflected back at her in Gerda's kind expression. They'd missed out on so much together. "That's so sweet of you. Thank you."

"You're welcome." Gerda gripped Desi's shoulders, letting her know how important this was to her.

Kent strolled up, stopping briefly when he realized he'd invaded a private moment. "Oh, sorry."

Desi and Gerda opened their hug but remained arm over arm. "Grandma just bought me the most beautiful sweater." The lady behind the counter had finished wrapping it in tissue paper and putting it inside a bag with all five of the Scandinavian flags on it, then handed it to Desi.

"That's great. You'll have to model it for me sometime." His genuine smile rolled over her, doubling the unfamiliar feelings she harbored in her heart right then, until caution stepped in. *Don't get too chummy with anyone because you won't be around that long.* At the warning, her arm slipped from her grandmother's back.

"I've got to get back to the booth," Gerda said. "Why don't you show Desi around all of the displays?"

"Glad to. That is, if Steven doesn't get his nose bent out of shape."

"I think he's forgotten me for that group of boys over there."

Gerda pointed at Kent. "I remember this one when he was Steven's age. I could tell he had a crush on Ester, and I warned her to be extra nice to him when she baby-sat. Do you remember that?"

"I do. Truth was, Ester was my first big heartbreak."

Kent went quiet as Gerda shut down before Desi's eyes. Pain replaced the tender glances from earlier, and after a goodbye nod, Gerda make a quick departure for the bakery booth.

Desi and Kent exchanged puzzled glances. How should she process what had just happened? Kent had accidentally brought up the taboo topic. No wonder it seemed so hard to ask about her mother, when her grandmother had never gotten over her running away.

Kent flattened his lips into a straight line. "I put my foot in it, didn't I?"

"It's so many years. Who would think it could still be so painful?"

"Losing a kid. I don't know how I'd survive," he said.

Desi couldn't begin to imagine the hurt her mother had caused when she'd set out on her own, barely eighteen and pregnant. Seemed as though there were always two sides to every story. Times like these, Desi wished with all of her heart her mother was alive and she could ask her the tough questions.

Kent glanced at his watch. "Well, it's after noon. The kid's distracted. Would you like a taste of schnapps in some cocoa? I know just the place."

"Sounds good." Anything to replace the heartsick feeling for her mother and grandmother that had suddenly come over her. How different would her life have been if her mother and grandparents could have worked things out?

Off they went, down the street toward a booth decorated in swaths the colors of the Swedish flag. On the way, without asking, Kent took her hand with a gentle, comforting touch, setting off a tingly domino effect all the way to her toes.

Chapter Three

Kent let rip a piercing whistle as he set the three co-
coas on the outdoor table. After Desi nearly jumped
from her chair, she saw Steven making a beeline for
them. The kid must know his dad's call.

"That's yours." Kent handed Desi a thick mug filled
with rich, hot chocolate with a strong peppermint aroma.

"Thanks." Seated beside a small round table, she
blew over the top of her mug and inhaled more of the
delicious scents. "You always call your kid like a dog?"

Kent winked at her. "Works every time."

The quick, subtle wink sent a comet up her spine,
and she sat infinitesimally straighter.

Steven arrived, took one quick sip and put the non-
spiked cocoa down. "Thanks, Dad! Gotta go."

"Wai…wai…wait a minute." Desi grabbed the boy's
sleeve and pulled him back. "I thought I was your guest
today. Stick around and finish your cocoa. Talk to us a

little bit before you run off with your friends again, or I'll get my feelings hurt."

The boy sat on the edge of the chair, too antsy to sit still. "We're playing tag." He slurped another drink. "I'm it."

"Sounds fun, but they get to see you every day at school." Once she had Steven's attention, she took a long drink of the warm, spiked cocoa and let it go down slow.

"Have you ever been in the parade?" she asked.

Steven tried to be polite, feet fidgeting, eyes darting to the side from time to time. "Not yet. But next year the fourth-grade class gets to make a float and wear costumes."

Desi glanced toward Kent. "Were you in the parade when you were in fourth grade?"

"You bet. One of the biggest days of my grammar school life." Kent's usual guarded style gave way to a smile, making him look younger, even a little carefree.

But Steven changed. His previous exuberance closed down and he stared at his drink. "Will I wear Swedish or Norwegian colors, Dad?"

"Both, if that's what you want to do."

Kent had grown more solemn, too, and Desi's imagination started working overtime. Swedish? Norwegian? Her eyes darted between father and son. Did it have something to do with the missing mother and wife? And what was the deal with her? But like so many other times, she left her questions unspoken.

Steven finished half of his drink and plopped the cup on the table. "Now can I go play?"

"What about me?" Desi teased, reaching to tickle his sweatshirt-covered chest, trying to lighten the mood again.

"I'll bring you some bubblegum after me and my friends go to the candy booth."

"Gee, thanks. I feel so special." She glanced at Kent. "I hope he didn't learn his dating techniques from you."

Steven's eyes lit up. "I know! I'll bring you some fruit-flavored SweeTarts."

Never in her life would she ask for SweeTarts, or for a kid to spend his money on her, but since it seemed like such a big deal to the boy, she cheered. "Yay!"

Kent got a funny look on his face and shook his head as Steven sped off.

"You are going to pay him back, right?" she asked. "I'd hate for your kid to spend all of his hard-earned allowance on me."

"Wouldn't that make it our date?"

She locked eyes with Kent, refusing to get lost in those arctic blues. "How about I pay you and make it Dutch?" She looked suspiciously around, wondering if it was okay to say *Dutch* in Heartlandia.

Tiny crinkles formed at the edges of his eyes, and Desi realized Kent was smiling again. "The other night he told me you smell like his favorite candy. That's why he's buying the SweeTarts for you."

She laughed. "SweeTarts?" She sniffed her wrists. "I guess my perfume does smell a little like candy."

She offered her wrist for Kent to try. He leaned forward and sniffed, his gaze walking from her wrist up her arm and connecting with her eyes. Zing. Heat jetted from her chest to her cheeks in record time. Feeling awkwardly aroused, she took her arm back and pretended to watch Steven run off.

"How funny he noticed," she muttered.

"He's a smart kid. A great kid."

"Agreed." She sipped more of the delicious enhanced cocoa and let the newly emerged sunshine further warm her tingling face.

Kent's fingers tapped her knuckles, setting off a second wave of shivers. "He came from a mixed marriage, you know."

She cocked her head in Kent's direction. The kid was a towhead.

He had a playful glint in his eyes. "His mother's Norwegian."

"Ah. Gee, it must have been hard with two extremely different cultures living under the same roof." She'd play along to see if he'd open up about the wife who was no longer in the picture.

Kent stretched out his long legs and crossed them at the ankles then took a long draw on his cocoa. "I can't tell you how many arguments we had whether to serve *lefse* or regular potato pancakes."

"You're kidding, right? What's *lefse?*"

"It's a very thin pancake made from potatoes. Looks kind of like a flour tortilla. Great stuff. Want to try some? There's a booth over there."

Her hand shot up. "I'm good. Thanks. Just ate half a dozen *aebleskiver,* and whatever that fishy thing you brought me was, remember? But I'll take another rain check."

He studied her face. When the man let down his guard, he could melt her with that gorgeous smile straight out of a magazine. The women in this town were probably all waiting in the shadows for him to give the high sign that he was on the market again.

Hadn't Gerda said he'd been divorced less than a year?

None of that mattered anyway, since Desi was only a tourist in town. Still, she wondered about the whole story, and the more he smiled at her, the more she wanted to know the down and dirty truth. Maybe she'd venture to ask?

Except he beat her to the punch with another topic.

"So when you're not visiting your grandmother, what do you do?"

"That's a tough question." She studied her ceramic mug, noticing fine cracks in the glaze. "I guess you could call me a jack-of-all-trades. I've waited tables and worked in bookstores. I've booked entertainment for a couple of clubs here and there, mostly acted as my mother's assistant and later as her agent." She took a sip, thinking how ditzy she must sound to a doctor. "I designed clothes for a retro girl group that was on the same circuit as my mother for a while. Being stuck in hotel rooms growing up, I got pretty good with sewing, mostly fixing my mom's costumes. She gave me a portable sewing machine for my birthday one year." She paused for a moment, remembering her excitement on that sweet-sixteen birthday, and how she'd wished there were more people to share it with. "I've done a few other la-di-da jobs, too, but I won't bore you with them. Anyway, you name it, I've probably tried it."

He didn't say anything, just sat there digesting her confession. Even though he was a doctor, she hadn't tried to embellish her eclectic résumé. Truth was, she'd never ventured beyond her high school equivalency, probably not very impressive to an M.D.

"So you're the artistic type." He rubbed his chin with his thumb and index finger, studying her as if she'd lost her clothes or something. His scrutiny made her squirm.

"I guess you could say that."

"What about that *la-di-da* part?"

She scrunched up her face, not understanding what he'd meant.

"Those other jobs—you know, 'you name it and I've probably tried it.' The ones you don't want to bore me with?"

Ahh. "I can assure you, everything I've ever done has been perfectly legal."

"Good to know." He sat back, thinking. "Where'd you go to college?"

"Uh, I didn't. My mother homeschooled me since we were always on the road, and by the time I could apply for college, I was really into the costume designing. So I skipped college that year, and the next year something else came up. I guess I just never got around to going."

He sat up straight. "Hey, we've got a great new community college right here."

"Is that right? Well, I won't be sticking around long enough to go to school here, but thanks for thinking—"

He shrugged a shoulder. "Why rule it out?"

School or sticking around? She finished her cocoa. "Why make any hard-and-fast plans? We'll see."

He didn't look satisfied with her answer, but what did she care?

Steven came barreling up to them again. "Here's your candy." He shoved it into her hands and took off again.

"Thanks," she shouted, positive the boy didn't hear her. She cocked her head. "Some date he turned out to be." When she glanced at Kent, there was that heart-melting smile again. Was it meant for her or because of Steven's antics? Or maybe because he could tell she genuinely liked his son.

"For my kid's sake, I hope you'll stick around awhile."

After all of his downright sexy smiles today, she wondered if maybe Kent wanted her to stick around, too. Or was this more about him being overprotective of his son and whoever the kid cared about not leaving?

Racking her brain, she couldn't remember anyone in her life ever asking her to stay put. Well, she had received an open-ended invitation from her grandmother to come to Heartlandia for as long as she wanted. That was one thing, but no *man* had ever seemed interested in anything long term. Not that she'd just taken an innocent comment from the gorgeous man across from her and blown it way out of proportion or anything. Talk about feeling needy. *Must be the schnapps.*

As much as she'd like to think Kent had sent a subtle message about sticking around in Heartlandia, she was savvy enough to know he was only being protective of his son. Desi looked deep into Kent's morning-sky stare and could have sworn there was a second part to that message she needed to decipher, and it all went back to his missing wife.

Kent finally got Steven to settle down and go to bed around nine o'clock. The kid had talked nonstop about *the best day of his life* after they'd dropped Desdemona back home. It gave Kent hope that Steven was coming out of his hurting place and that life would get better. For both of them.

It had been a big day, and the boy had a lot to process: his new piano teacher, who had lavished him with attention and made him blush; the civic-pride event of the year; running with his friends downtown. How free he must have felt, and it had been a long time since Kent had seen him cut loose like that.

Hell, last year they'd skipped the festival altogether, Kent making the excuse he had to work. He'd made sure he was scheduled just to avoid it.

Amazingly, even tonight, Steven's unending desire to impress Ms. Desi had led him to practice his piano lessons before taking his bath. That earnest look of concentration brought a swell of love so strong that Kent almost had to sit down. He shook his head over how a pretty woman could get a guy, even at the tender age of eight, to do things he'd never do on his own.

This wasn't good. Steven would go and get attached to her—the lady who couldn't even commit to sticking around long enough to enroll in college—and then she'd leave…just like Steven's mother had. Yet Kent couldn't bring himself to put a stop to it. He liked seeing the joy on his son's face again. He understood the lure of the new, mysterious woman. She'd gotten to him, too.

Kent loved seeing his kid smile, and he liked having a little pizzazz added back into their routine. But as with everything in life, this would come with a price. Maybe Desdemona would stick around, continue to teach piano, take some classes at the city college. It wasn't as if he had any control over it or not. But God knew Gerda would love to keep her here and could use her help, especially now that she'd agreed to fill in as mayor and the election wasn't for months yet.

Kent ventured out front to get some air, using the excuse of double-checking whether he'd locked up the truck or not. His gaze wandered to the large front window at the Rask house. The lights were bright, and inside, Desi walked back and forth, talking on a cell phone.

She'd let her hair down and wore a colorful dress that looked more like a scarf. It hung to the floor and clung to her full-proportioned body, and he couldn't help but notice when the light hit her just right, she was braless.

An almost forgotten response wound its way into his chest, down his torso and through his hips. Damn, she was good-looking. *Careful, Larson. Don't let her beauty mess with your head.* How many times today had he admired her light bronze complexion, the sprinkling of freckles across her nose and those rich dark eyes? Not to mention the lush lips begging to be— He shook his head. *Think straight. She lives hand to mouth, picks up jobs here and there, doesn't stick with any particular thing for long. She's spent her life traveling the country, never settling down. She's just passing through.*

His fists opened and closed as he did battle with the two strongest organs in his body. His brain knew without a doubt she'd break Steven's heart. More than anything Kent wanted to protect his son, but he knew life had a way of playing out in the least expected ways. Why deprive the kid of the dazzling Ms. Desi?

Why deprive himself?

It took a lot of discipline, but he broke his gaze from Desdemona and strode toward the truck.

He thought briefly about canceling Steven's next lesson if Desi was going to teach. But no way would Steven let him; hell, he'd never been more motivated or prepared. Why rob the boy of his enjoyment and reward from hard work? It had been a long time since he'd seen his son so animated and carefree. In some crazy way, maybe Desdemona could be part of the healing process instead of the purveyor of more grief.

He shoved fingers through his hair, and through the

car window he stole one last, quick look at Desi. Damn, the sight of her got to him again. Yet she was the exact opposite of what he needed in his life right now. There he went, overanalyzing. Whatever warm and sexy feelings he'd allowed to slip through just now had been successfully, surgically removed. As usual.

He strangled the handle on the truck with his grip, frustrated. *For once, Larson, can't you just go with the flow?*

He jimmied the cold metal, ensured the car was locked, made an about-face and marched back into the house without another glance next door. But the image of Desdemona was already implanted in his mind... every last detail. No bra.

The next day Kent rushed home late again, having way too many patients at the Urgent Care for the allotted time slots. He really needed to learn to stick with his appointment schedule. This was the third time in two weeks he'd had to ask his babysitter to stay an extra hour.

The sitter's car was parked out front, so he pulled the truck into the driveway, noticing Desdemona sitting on the front porch again. She wasn't looking his way or he would have waved. He rushed up the steps to the front door and let himself into the half-dark house.

Amanda sat with Steven at the kitchen table, helping him with homework.

"I'm sorry I'm late again." He didn't bother to check the mail, just went right to the kitchen. "I'll take over the homework from here."

"No need, Mr. Larson. Steven's all done."

Steven closed his book, making a loud clap.

"Hi, Dad. Can I watch some TV now?"

"A half hour. That's all. I'll have dinner ready by then." Kent started for the cupboards. What the heck did he have around to feed Steven?

"I already fed him," Amanda said, gathering her things.

"Hey, thanks."

"I was starving. She made me two hot dogs." Antsy as always, Steven acted as if he needed a bathroom, quick.

"You're always starving." He leaned against the counter.

"I should get to watch an hour of TV 'cause I already practiced piano, too."

"He did really well." Amanda seemed as surprised as Kent had been at first. Piano practice wasn't something the boy had ever been consistent about.

"I'm all ready for my lesson tomorrow." Pride puffed out his chest as he stood and headed for the TV room. "I'll play my song for you later, Dad."

"Good job, bud."

Kent walked Amanda out front, already hearing the TV loud and clear on Steven's favorite kid sitcom. The past couple of days had warmed up considerably, and he'd missed all the sunshine being stuck inside at work, and since a certain someone happened to be sitting outside earlier, he thought…

Amanda waved and drove off. Kent glanced to Gerda's porch but couldn't see Desdemona anymore. Blast it, his timing stank. He moved a little closer and searched the porch. Two wine-barrel planters stocked with summer blooms marked each end of it. A large fern hung from the arch over the railing, blocking the entire view from this vantage point.

His gaze drifted to the far corner. Boots rested on the railing and they were connected to Desi. She sat in the rocking chair, staring straight at him. Damn. Busted.

Surveillance was Gunnar's talent, not his. He waved at her in the shadows and approached with a sudden rush of excitement coursing through him.

"Nice night, huh?" he said.

"Actually feels like summer's coming. In L.A. we'd already be using air-conditioning." She held something in her hand. "Hey, now that you're off duty, maybe you'd like to join me for a wine cooler? My own secret concoction."

Surprisingly, he liked the idea. "Sounds good. Where's Gerda?"

Desi stood, and Kent got treated to an up-close view of that sexy multicolored scarf dress she seemed to like to lounge around in. Something about the clunky boots beneath made her look edgy and he liked the effect.

"She had to go to some hush-hush meeting with the city council."

Knowing Steven was set for at least the next half hour, he followed her inside. The screen door creaked and flapped behind them. Walking quickly across the large living area, they were soon in the kitchen. Desi mixed Japanese plum wine with club soda over ice, then refreshed her tall glass and handed him both of the drinks. She stopped at the couch and picked up a large, long pillow, carrying it outside and placing it on the top porch step so they could both sit on it together. Out here he could keep an eye on his house in case Steven needed him.

Desdemona sat first and patted the spot next to her. He'd never been this close to her before and didn't need to be asked twice.

He took a drink. It was bubbly, tart, yet with a sweet aftertaste. "This is very good."

"Tell me about it. Problem is, they sneak up on you." Desi seemed more relaxed than he'd ever seen her, and after his long, stressful day he had some catching up to do.

They sat in silence, enjoying the drinks, and he studied the clear starlit sky, the Columbia River sparkling in the distance. Wind rustled through the front-yard trees and breezed over his face. He could smell the pine trees all the way from the hills behind town. He took another drink and relaxed a bit more. A sudden gust of wind kicked up some leaves, lifting Desdemona's hair every which way. He turned to watch the show.

Had he ever seen such soft-looking skin before? It would be so easy to reach over and kiss her. Instead he moved a lock of windblown hair from her face and tucked it behind her ear.

Desdemona gave a bashful, endearing smile. "Thank you."

Thump. It went right to Kent's heart. He fantasized tracing his finger along her back and kissing her neck— her long, beautiful neck.

The wind stopped and the air between them went thick, expectant.

She shivered.

He looked away, afraid she might notice the sex-starved thoughts written all over his face. Just because he was intensely drawn to her, he didn't want to make her uncomfortable.

"How's Steven?"

Safe topic. *Okay, we'll keep things safe.* "Great. He's all ready for his lesson tomorrow, which is a first."

"I love it." She drank several swallows of her wine cooler. Kent almost finished his.

"Yeah, dangle a pretty lady in front of any warm-blooded male and that's what you get."

Desdemona hitched her head, pulled in her chin and studied him. There was amusement in her expression, with a raised eyebrow of disbelief tossed in to balance things out. "Was that a compliment?"

"You don't know you're hot?"

She blurted a laugh. "I didn't know *you* thought I was hot."

"Am I alive?" He finished off his drink, staring straight ahead, hoping she wouldn't notice he'd felt about as awkward as a teenager.

She tapped his shoulder. He turned to find a mischievous twinkle in her eye. "Want another?" She'd noticed.

He didn't want to break up the moment, so he shook his head, though the easy-down-the-hatch drink had already tweaked his outlook. This going-with-the-flow stuff wasn't half-bad.

"Since we talked the other day, I've really been wondering about all those other jobs you've had," he said, thinking, by habit, he'd already put a stop to the go-with-the-flow bit. Maybe she had office experience and he could get her a job at his Urgent Care.

"The odds-and-ends jobs?"

Did he really want to know or was he just making stuff up so that now he'd finished his drink he could stick around and look at her more? "Yeah, those."

"I'm a calligrapher and have some pretty good accounts. I know computers can do that stuff these days, but there's nothing like the real thing. Plenty of people still want it, and it brings in decent money." She scratched her chin. "And the last job I had before I came here was at the senior center in L.A. where my mother and I lived."

"That's nice. What did you do there?"

"I posed for the Life Art classes."

"Hmm. Did they dress you in different costumes when you posed?"

"No." She acted blasé and moved her large-eyed glance toward Kent's face in a lazy fashion. "I posed nude." She used her straw to take a long draw on her drink, eyes unwavering from his.

He almost choked. "You what?"

"Pose naked." She blew a puff of air from between her lips, pulled at the seams of the pillow and punched the fluffy filling down a tad, then relaxed into the cushion. "Hey, there isn't anyone under sixty in the class and they're mostly women. Besides, it's for art."

"Aren't you self-conscious about people staring at you naked?"

"Maybe at first, but it's artistic and I feel a little daring doing it. You know, out of the ordinary."

So she didn't do ordinary, which was all Kent and Steven were. Diana had gotten tired of ordinary, too.

Still, that daring part she'd mentioned got his full attention and he let himself look her over head to booted toes, stuttering over her chest. How had he not noticed before now that she was braless again? He quickly diverted his gaze to his hands, making a fist with one and butting it against the other palm.

"Don't go getting any weird notions about me. The

first time I posed I nearly puked, but I'm not uptight about my body."

"Good to know." Okay, he was feeling his drink but things still seemed awkward. Maybe because he'd been transported back in time to a horny teenager.

"Maybe we should keep this between us. I wouldn't want to cause my mayor grandma any scandals. She's only just getting to know me." There was a touch of sassy in her grin, and he made a snap decision that he really liked Desi's brand of sassy.

"My, my, my." Kent grinned back his own version of a sassy smile and leaned on his elbows, happy to finally find the relaxation he'd needed, compliments of the plum wine and Ms. Desdemona Rask.

She leaned back on her elbows, too. Her hair fell below her shoulders as she scanned the night sky. The curve of her throat and soft full breasts below demanded his attention. He swallowed. Damn, he should never have come over here.

On impulse he lifted the mahogany-colored hair off the shoulder closest to him, feeling the thick, wavy texture.

She closed her eyes.

Crazy vibes whizzed up his arm and across his shoulders.

He either needed to kiss her or leave. Some deep, honorable part of his subconscious put on the brakes, but the urge to test out her inviting lips, just a few inches away, overrode that hesitation.

Kent reached across her chest to her shoulder and turned her toward him. Their eyes met—hers with a knowing, warm and welcoming glance. He locked into her dark, sexy gaze until his lips made contact with hers and his lids closed.

Soft. Plump. Warm. Her lips were everything he'd thought and more. He tasted the plum wine as he deepened the kiss, and her fingers delved into his hair.

The kiss set off sensations and desires he'd buried since Diana had left. Hot-blooded desire. He wanted Desdemona, and he wasn't sure what to do about it. From the way she kissed him back, he was positive she was on board, too.

When his tongue crossed the seams of her lips and he touched the tip of hers, he quit thinking. He let his mind wander with the zero-to-ninety rush of making out with this beautiful woman.

Desdemona ended it. She pulled away and stared into his eyes. It took him a moment to focus. "That was nice." Her voice was breathy. Sexy. Oozing sincerity.

Only nice? Hell. He feigned a smile, fighting off the lance to his ego. "I can blame the plum wine if that makes things easier to explain."

"What would you blame it on otherwise?"

Tell her the truth. "Your irresistibleness."

A whispery laugh parted her lips. "Is that even a word?" Her sweet, questioning expression proved she liked his attention.

"It is if it's true."

She gazed dreamily at him, those dark topaz eyes so warm and inviting, like the night. She'd liked it. Definitely. Should he kiss her again?

Desi relaxed back on the step, staring in the direction of the river. Kent rested his elbows on his knees and gave her space.

"You know, part of the reason I came to Oregon was to find my biological father."

They'd broken the ice with the intimate kiss, and he liked how she was opening up with him. "Is he from around here?"

"No. I believe he lives in Portland. My mother only told me about him when she was dying. I feel like I've got to find him. Sort of like finding the other half of me."

Kent's jaw went tight. "What about Gerda?"

"Oh, I plan to stay long enough to get to know her. I'll keep her in my life for sure, yet…"

And there you go, Larson—the reason you shouldn't get involved with her.

"Dad?" A distant voice cut further into Kent's suddenly aborted trip to pleasantville. "Are you out here? It's time for my bath."

Kent stood. Even now, after the realization his attraction to Desi couldn't go anywhere, his natural and red-blooded reaction to that kiss proved embarrassing. Good thing it was getting dark out.

"Well, I gotta go. Kid's calling," he said, sounding husky, maybe a little frustrated, and way out of practice when it came to women.

Desi stood on the steps, watching him leave, looking like a booted, scarf-covered goddess, the kind that should pose for a painting. Light from the house outlined her figure through the thin, almost transparent material of her dress. A new gust of wind rustled the hem of her skirt as she waved good-night with a smoldering smile. The sight almost made his knees buckle.

"Dad!"

"Co—" He needed to clear his throat. "Coming."

Going to see Desdemona had been a wonderfully terrible idea. He backed away from the porch, rubbing his neck. Why did everything in life have to be so complicated?

"Hi, Ms. Desi!"

"Hey there, Steven."

With a final wave good-night, Kent made his getaway…quick.

Chapter Four

On Tuesday, Steven trotted across Gerda's lawn with his babysitter hot on his heels. Desi saw them through the front window and hopped off the piano bench, leaving her current student fumbling through a song.

"Keep playing, Dagney." She opened the door before he could knock. "You're early."

"I know!" He stood there in his summer-day-camp clothes, mud on the knees of his jeans and face grimy with sweat and dirt streaks.

"I tried to distract him by taking him to the park, but he's been chomping at the bit to get here for the last half hour," said the young woman she'd seen come and go as the babysitter.

Seeing Steven set off all kinds of thoughts, mainly about his father and their amazing kiss, but also what a sweet boy he was to get so excited about his lesson. She'd hardly been able to keep Kent out of her thoughts today and was thankful for the piano-teaching distractions. Seeing Steven set her progress in reverse.

"Why don't you wait right here on the porch—" she pointed to the wicker love seat "—and I'll get to you as soon as Dagney is finished."

The pent-up excitement leaked from his face, his expression going flat. "Okay."

"It'll only be a few more minutes." She ruffled his damp hair and closed the door then sat beside Dagney, who'd stopped playing to watch what was going on.

"Sorry about the interruption. Let's start right here." Desi pointed to the middle of the page.

Ten minutes later, Desi sent Dagney home and let Steven in. He ran for the piano bench, slipping on a braided area rug on the way, almost hitting the floor on his knees. Using quick reflexes, Desi grabbed him by the elbow before he went down. They smiled at each other and after he'd calmed down they sat side by side on the piano bench.

After the warm-ups and some theory talk, they got down to the lesson.

"Wow, you even did your theory homework," she said, thumbing through the workbook.

Pride could not adequately describe the joy on his face when she put gold stickers on all of the pages. Knowing he was practically blowing a gasket trying to be patient, she pushed ahead. "Okay, play your new song for me."

The boy sat tall, placing his fingers on the keyboard, wrists straight and slightly lifted, then began the blues song. A few notes in, Desi realized he was playing from memory, and the improvement over last week was amazing. Gerda had asked Desi to light a fire under the boy's feet for music, and she definitely felt as though that mission had been accomplished.

She called her grandmother to come and witness the miracle. Gerda clapped her hands in delight. "He deserves two candies this week," she said, before giving him a hug and retreating to the back of the house to make more work-related phone calls. It didn't go unnoticed that she'd given Desi freedom to teach in her own style.

Steven gave his all to the rest of the lesson, too, and when Desi added a few new notes and chords to his music, he paid unwavering attention. Night and day from last week. By the end of the hour, Desi had introduced another short bluesy song for him to try on his own.

"This one's even cooler than the last one," he said, after her demonstration.

"I can't wait to see how you do." After putting bright stickers on his music pages, she handed him an extra-special candy, a small bag of SweeTarts, the tropical kind. She'd had a hunch he was going to nail the lesson today and decided to be prepared. "Now that I know how much you like SweeTarts, I bought some for the really great lessons."

His bright sky-blue eyes shone with pure delight, and he hugged her, giving it his all, just like he'd given to the piano lesson. The doorbell rang and, not wanting to break up the hug by answering the door, she called out, "Come in!"

In came Kent, nearly stunning her with his classic masculine looks. He wore charcoal slacks and a yellow button-down shirt, cuffs rolled to his forearms displaying strength and sophistication. His dark blond hair was slicked back with hair product, except the slightly longer hair on his neck curled out a tiny bit. Normally she'd make a guy out to be more than he actually was in her memory, and would inevitably be disappointed the next time she saw him, but not so with Kent. Every time they came face-to-face he only got better looking. The man had to be related to the Nordic gods, and his near perfection proved it.

Don't be so superficial. He's a great father, too. And a doctor for the town.

"Hi," he said, looking tentative and withdrawn, totally different from the last time she'd seen him.

What was she supposed to make of Kent's spine-melting kiss? She'd stood on the steps watching him go home last night, hardly able to believe the guy had made a pass at her. No one should let his bland white house fool them, because the man gave smokin'-hot kisses. Yet right now he seemed reserved, maybe even unhappy. Why? Was he sorry he'd kissed her?

"Hi." She gave him a bright smile, hoping to lighten the serious look on Kent's face. "Steven had a stellar lesson."

"Good to know." He nodded and smiled at his son.

Steven shot her a look as if he couldn't wait to crow about how well he'd done. "She said I did everything perfect, Dad!"

"Fantastic." Kent's smile didn't reach anywhere near his eyes. He didn't venture beyond the doorframe, either.

Steven let go of Desi, breaking up their hug, then rushed toward his dad, music books long forgotten. Kent gave him a jock's pat on the butt as he barreled straight out the door.

"I want to try the new song all by myself. See you, Ms. Desi!" From the sound of his voice he'd already cleared the porch and was halfway across the yard.

Desi cupped her hands around her mouth. "You won't get far without your music books."

In he ran, retrieving the music primers, and he sped right back out the door again.

"Call me if you need any help," she said as he disappeared again.

That left Kent and Desi alone, quietly staring at each other. Warmth edged up her throat to her jaw. She smiled, even though her right cheek felt a little twitchy.

"Mind if I ask you a favor?" Kent said after their silence had stretched into the uncomfortable stage.

"Not at all," she said with a sudden hopeful feeling. Would he ask her out, just the two of them, maybe for that midnight supper? Hopefully, if he did, he'd be in a better mood.

One large hand pulled free from his back pocket and he scratched the corner of his eyebrow. "I was wondering if you could back off a little from Steven."

She couldn't stop herself from pulling in her chin. "But we've been getting along so great and he's made phenomenal progress in one week."

"I know. That's great and all, but his heart is fragile right now. Please try to understand."

She bit back the load of questions in her mind, choosing the most obvious. "Does this have something to do with your kissing me?"

"No. I really liked doing that." Some life had come into his pensive eyes, and she breathed a little easier. "Having to ask you to back off from my son, not so much."

"Then why do it?" Desi shook her head and studied her shoes.

"It's a long story. I shouldn't dump it on you."

Must have something to do with Steven's mother not being around. It really isn't any of my business.

"Look, Steven and I get along great, and I don't understand why you want to put a stop to that, but you're the father, and I'll try to understand."

"Thank you. And I'm not trying to put a stop to anything. It's just he's a little too eager for attention these days. Too needy. It's my job to protect him." He leaned his shoulder against the doorframe, arms folded, without offering further explanation.

"From me?"

By the set of his jaw, she could tell an answer wouldn't be forthcoming. Frustrated, she asked, "You always this way?"

"Am I being a jerk?"

"Borderline." At least he had a clue. It made her smile. "You're being all mysterious. Hot and kissing me one minute. Asking me to back off from your kid the next."

"I don't mean to be." And by his withdrawn posture, he definitely didn't want to get into a discussion.

"Well, you haven't exactly been the most sensitive guy in town, running hot one time, cold the next." She hoped she could egg him on, get him to talk.

He opened his mouth but just as quickly closed it. Whatever he'd wanted to say hadn't evidently been worth the effort. If she were standing closer, frustrated as she was, she might have kicked his shin to help him along.

"Look, I'm glad Steven loves his piano lessons. It's just…" He battled inside, his eyes darting around the room as if searching for the words he couldn't quite make himself say. "Not a good time. I've got to go."

"Well, if you're hoping Gerda will be teaching the lesson next week, I can't guarantee it. Her arthritis is still bad, some of her finger joints are swollen and she's got a whole other responsibility as mayor."

And I think she's really enjoying the break. Plus, it lets me feel like I'm paying my way staying here.

"Just try to stop making Steven think you're the greatest person he's ever met."

"Didn't realize I was doing that." Again he cast her a perplexed look. He really was confused. "Are you jealous?"

"Not at all. I think you're great, too."

"Then why do I have to be different for your kid?"

He shoved his hands into his pockets and took a slow breath. "Because I asked you to."

"You're asking me to not be me. I can't help responding to him. He's a sweet and wonderful kid."

Kent backed out the doorway. "And you're a fantastic teacher." He gave her an earnest glance, as if begging her to understand the big mysterious reason he refused to share. "I'm sure you'll think of a way to remain professional without being his best friend."

He left, and the screen door flapped closed.

She stared after him, her jaw dropping. "What the hell just happened?" Had she imagined her time on the porch with Kent last night? No way could she make up that kiss. Nope. It had been real, hot and sexy, and it had set off sparks in out-of-the-way places. She'd been positive he'd felt it, too.

Desi planted her fist on her hip, ticked off and confused, staring at the empty doorway. If everyone in

Heartlandia was as hard to figure out as Kent Larson, she couldn't wait to move on.

She strode to the back of the house to the den, where she knew Gerda would be. Through with her calls, her grandmother sat on a small classic love seat watching an antiquated, tiny TV.

"What is the deal with that Kent Larson? One minute he invites me to the parade—" she kept the kiss part to herself "—the next he tells me to keep away from his kid. How am I supposed to do that when I give Steven piano lessons?"

After hearing Desi's gripes, Gerda looked alarmed. "Oh, no. Sounds like things backfired."

"What do you mean by 'things'?"

"You've really gotten through to Steven, and I can tell how much he likes you. You've gotten through to Kent, too, if the way he looked at you the other day at the parade meant anything." Gerda went thoughtfully quiet, her kind eyes drifting from the TV to Desi. "I think he's scared."

Desi sat on the edge of the love seat, needing to get to the bottom of this mystery. "Why? What about me could scare Kent?" *I know I'm a different shade than most everyone else in Heartlandia, but he had no problem with that when he kissed me.*

Gerda turned off the TV and gave Desi all of her attention. "It's not you he's scared of. It's about Steven getting attached to you. The boy lost his mother last year."

The information, out of the blue, felt like a sucker punch. "You make it sound like she died instead of getting divorced."

Gerda grew quiet, pulled inward for a couple of seconds. "She left."

Desi caught her breath. "Left?" It wasn't often a woman left her family. How bad could being married to Kent have been?

"She was a selfish one. Always had been. And willful. Always had to have her way, and in case you haven't noticed, Kent is a domineering kind of guy. They were always banging heads. Then one day instead of working things out she up and left."

A heartsick feeling hung heavy in Desi's chest. She could understand leaving a man, but how did a woman leave her child, too?

"No visits?"

"Nothing. She severed all contact, gave Kent full custody. Nearly broke Kent in two, but he keeps going because he has to. For the boy."

"Was there…abuse?"

Gerda shook her head with confidence. "Kent is a healer, not a hurter. The woman just didn't want to be married and have those responsibilities anymore, I guess."

There had to be more to it than that.

Sadness enveloped Desi. No wonder Kent had a chip on his shoulder and didn't want Steven to get attached to her. He knew she didn't plan to stick around for long. And she hadn't been the least bit concerned letting him know it, either. He'd been feeling her out by mentioning the city college and she'd blown that suggestion right out of the water.

Oh, God, poor Steven. And Kent—big, strong, gorgeous Kent. Desi needed a serious attitude adjustment in regards to the tall, stubborn doc next door. Since she didn't have a clue how to handle the situation, she'd avoid him. Let things be. After the message he'd delivered today, it should suit him just fine.

A quick replay of their kiss gave her pause. She didn't want to avoid him; she'd hoped to know him better, see where this crazy out-of-the-blue attraction might lead. But it wouldn't be fair to get involved with the man or his son because she really did have plans to leave. And evidently, they'd both already had enough of that.

She glanced at her grandmother, patted her bony hand. "Thanks for sharing."

"Of course, dear."

How similar Kent's wife's story sounded to her mother's, running off from loved ones to find a bigger life outside of quaint Heartlandia. Did the comparison stab at the old wound? Desi suddenly needed to hug her grandmother, and Gerda was completely receptive to the gesture.

As they hugged, Desi thought of her biological father. She needed to find him to put the last pieces of her life puzzle together. Until she was whole, she wouldn't have anything to offer anyone, especially not to that big galoot and his darling kid next door.

Wednesday morning, with loads of free time on her hands, Desi ventured back into town. Thanks to the parade and her afternoon spent with Kent, she had her bearings straight. She parked on Heritage Street, smack in the middle of the downtown area. The first thing she wanted to check out was the town monument and city hall. After all, she couldn't resist seeing where Gerda had been going for all of the hush-hush meetings the past week.

After a brisk two-block walk, she circled around a grassy knoll where the magnificent granite monument took center stage. The sculpture looked like a totem pole except it was made out of rock. It depicted ships and fishermen and native peoples intertwined and working together. The top looked like the tower part of a lighthouse, complete with a lantern. The inscription read "Working together for a better life. Heartlandia, founded 1750."

She wandered down the main street where the parade had been, noticing storefront after storefront, each more adorable than the last. How could such a small town support so many bakeries, knitting shops, bookstores and memento marts?

Squinting into the bright sun, she glanced into the distance toward the huge Columbia River. Down by the docks sat a humongous cruise ship. It had entered the port late last night after one long horn blast, which woke her up about three in the morning. Ah, so the tourist trade was big in these parts.

She'd had trouble going back to sleep after the horn, so here she was, wandering around the heart of downtown Heartlandia, bright and early when most of the businesses weren't even open. She glanced up to the backdrop of the hillside covered in trees and eclectically designed houses that Gerda had said got passed from one generation to the next.

She went inside a bakery called Fika with blue-and-white awnings and curtains to match and ordered a cup of coffee and a croissant. After, sitting out front, she buttered up her breakfast and ate the delicious fluffy treat, sipping bold-tasting coffee in between and scouting out the other buildings.

Her gaze came to rest on that redbrick-fronted restaurant and bar, the place where the older African-American man had greeted her on Saturday. Once she'd finished her quickie breakfast, she headed back to Lincoln's Place for a closer look.

It was closed, which was what she'd expected at this hour, but she put her face to the window, hands blocking the sun at her temples, and peered inside for a better look. There was a white piano smack in the middle of the restaurant area, which was kitty-corner to the huge wraparound wood bar. Behind the bar on the wall, and placed where everyone could see, was a portrait of Abraham Lincoln.

Movement in her peripheral vision caught her eye. It was the man she'd seen the other day, and he was waving her in. How embarrassing getting caught snooping in his window. She couldn't very well pretend she didn't notice him, though she wanted to cut and run. She waved back, and he motioned for her to come inside.

The man met her at the door, unlocking it and inviting her inside.

"I'm Cliff Lincoln, the proprietor of this establishment. Come in. And you are?"

"Desdemona Rask, but everyone calls me Desi."

"I like Desdemona better. Mind if I call you that?"

She shook her head. "So I'm new in town, and—"

"Don't I know that. You and me kind of stand out around here."

The way he spoke, like melting butter coating his words, made her smile. By the salt-and-pepper short, tight hair, he looked to be in his fifties, but he hardly had creases on his face. Whether from a life well lived or simply good genes, she didn't know, but something had worked in his favor.

Tall with evidence around the middle of a life centered on good food, he led her toward the bar. She sat on a stool, admiring the rich dark wood with intricately carved inlays. A mishmash of bench-type tables and chairs filled the rest of the casual area, but the dining room shifted into a cleaner, upscale style with black lacquered tables and chairs, white tablecloths and fresh flowers in crystal vases. The white baby grand piano divided the two diverse areas.

Without asking, he passed her a cup of fresh coffee and a few creamer containers. It would be her second cup of the day, but she didn't want to be impolite, so she weakened the strong brew with creamer.

"What brings you to these parts?" He leaned on his forearms on the bar and joined her with a cup of coffee.

"My mother grew up here. She died last year and asked me to come here to get to know my grandmother, so here I am."

"What do you think so far?"

"It's nice. My grandmother's really sweet."

"Good. Good."

"Are you from here?"

"Nope." He glanced out the window toward the Columbia River. "I used to be a chef on one of those cruise ships you may have noticed down at the docks. This stop was my favorite of all the cities. I got to know the previous owner of this place, whose name was also Lincoln. Fifteen years ago he wanted to retire and offered this place to me for a sweet price. I've been the only black man in town ever since, and no one has ever said a peep about it."

"That's wonderful. Are you married?"

"I've got a Danish wife and a couple of beautiful daughters."

Desi figured the mixed-race young girl in the parade the other day must have been his daughter. "That's great." She also wondered what it might have been like to be that mixed-raced girl in the parade twenty years ago, when people may have peeped a lot about it. But that was all a moot point, since her mother had never intended to go home again.

"You like soul food?" His question snapped her out of her thoughts.

"I always have it on the menu," he said, "for the daring types on cruises. Plus some of my regulars have come to expect it, too. If you want I can whip up some grits and fried okra?"

"Oh, no, thanks."

"Collard greens?"

"I'm good, thanks. Just had a croissant. Bit early for lunch."

"You don't eat soul food, do you." It wasn't a question.

She shook her head again, feeling a little embarrassed. "Not really."

"Cain't say you've lived until you've had my sweet-potato pie."

She couldn't resist his raised brows and friendly dare. "That does sound good." The man was being kind and generous, and even though she'd just had a croissant she didn't want to be impolite. "I'll take a tiny sliver if you've got some on hand."

"You got it. I always come in early to bake my pies." He went back in the kitchen to get the pie and she wandered over to the white piano, lifted the lid and uncovered the keys, then tapped a few notes. The instrument had beautiful tone.

"You play?" Cliff said, holding two plates with something much bigger than a sliver of pie on each.

"Yes. My mother was an accomplished pianist. She taught me. I'm not as good as her, but not so bad, either."

"Feel free to try it out. I bought that from a pianist from the cruise ship. He said he used to hang out with Liberace. Do you even know who he is?"

She nodded. "Sure I do. So where's the candelabra?"

A rich deep laugh rolled out of his chest.

She played one of her favorite Duke Ellington songs, "Do Nothing Till You Hear From Me," and added an extra-bluesy touch for Cliff.

He grinned and ate his pie while she played. When she'd finished, he clapped and brought her pie over then sat on the piano bench with her. "You want a job? I could use some nice dinner music like that on the weekends."

Did she want to follow in her mother's footsteps? It had been a tough life for both her and her mother. "That's awfully kind of you, but I'm helping my grandma with her piano students right now, and I'm not sure how long I'll be in town…." She took a bite of his sweet potato pie and took a quick trip to pie heaven. "Mmm-mm, this is good."

"I'm tryin' to tell you."

She smiled and covered her mouth. "If I worked here, you could pay me in pie."

"You could use some meat on your bones, too."

She snorted a laugh. Then why did she always feel fuller-sized than other women? "Right." She loved how relaxed Cliff made her feel, and for an instant she honestly thought about taking him up on his offer. What if?

After the last bite, she handed him the plate and thanked him. "I've got to go, and you probably need to get ready for the lunch crowd." She'd heard a few people arrive back in the kitchen, and pots and pans started clinking and clanking behind the swinging doors. "I'll think about your offer. I promise."

He showed her to the entrance. "Don't be scarce, girl. You know where to find me."

"It was nice to meet you, Mr. Lincoln."

"You, too, Desdemona. And call me Cliff like all my friends do."

She walked back to her car feeling as though she'd just made a friend, and how working part-time for a friend could help him out as much as her. But accepting the job would mean sticking around, and she needed to find her father before she could stick around anywhere. Cliff would understand that.

On Sunday, Grandma Gerda spent the whole day preparing dinner. The *gravet laks,* salmon, had been cold-cured and ready to serve as an appetizer. The batter for the *lefse,* potato pancakes, was ready for pouring and grilling. Desi's least favorite vegetable on the planet, beets, was pickled and cold. Somehow, she would manage at least one bite so as not to insult her grandmother. But it was the thought of the main meal, roasted lamb chops with mushrooms and barley, that made her mouth water.

Her mother's older brother, Uncle Erik, and his wife, Helena, would be there. Admittedly nervous about meeting relatives she never knew she had, Desi dressed up.

She wore a gray, high-waist, straight skirt with a bright yellow top that dipped a bit too low for a family meal, so she added a white, lacy camisole. She even put on her dress-up pumps, making her a little self-conscious about her height. She'd decided to wear her hair down and, since she wanted to make a good impression, she wore a little more makeup than usual.

At four o'clock Desi set the table for six, as instructed, assuming she had a couple of cousins she'd be meeting, too, then she joined her grandmother in the kitchen to watch a master at work on the main dish.

Gerda already had the barley cooked and waiting in a grainy mountain inside a stainless-steel dish.

"Chop this for me, would you?" Gerda handed Desi a pile of green leaves.

"What's this?"

"Kale. It's good for you."

Of all of the ingredients, this large, thick-veined leaf looked the least appetizing.

Meanwhile, Gerda minced onion and garlic like a TV chef, tossing it into a huge pan to brown.

"So what does Uncle Erik do?"

"He works for a big internet company in the insurance department, and they've sent him all over the world. You would have met him before now, but he and his wife just got back from Japan."

"And my cousins?"

"Oh, they're all grown and living across the country. Anni lives in Maine. She teaches school, and Christoffer lives in Washington, near the Canadian border. He's a journalist for an online newspaper."

"Wow, and they came this far just to meet me?"

"Oh, no, sorry—Anni and Chris won't be here tonight."

"But I set the table for six."

Gerda turned back to the counter and chopped a pile of brown mushrooms as if she were being timed. "I invited Kent and Steven."

Desi's blossoming appetite vanished, her stomach tightening. Kent? How was she supposed to face him over dinner and not be reminded of their kiss? And how in the world was she supposed to honor his request to back off from Steven, when they kept being thrown together?

Why had he even accepted Gerda's offer?

She was nervous enough about meeting long-lost relatives, and now the thought of sharing a meal with family and a sexy new neighbor seemed impossible.

Before she could worry another second, the doorbell rang.

Chapter Five

From the kitchen, Desi ran her suddenly moist hands down the front of her skirt and crossed beside the dining table and through the living room to answer the door. Seeming as nervous as Desi was, Gerda followed right on her heels.

When Desi opened the door, it wasn't Kent and Steven as she'd thought, but her uncle and aunt. Immediately, her butterflies shifted into another kind of jitters.

"Erik," Gerda cooed. "It's so good to see you. Come in. Come in." The tall, thin man, with blond hair morphing into silver, ducked to hug and kiss his mother—the family resemblance unmistakable.

A heavyset brunette waited her turn to say hello, and Gerda kissed her daughter-in-law's cheek. "Helena, you look beautiful as always." The woman's red-lipstick smile made Desi grin.

"And I know you've both been eager to meet our

Desdemona." Gerda nudged Desi forward, since she'd been hanging back, feeling a little shy.

Erik and Helena both gave her polite hugs of welcome, genuine smiles on their faces. Moisture brimmed in Erik's eyes and she could tell hers were doing the same. No doubt her mother's running away had left many hearts and minds hurt and confused for years and years. Desi was probably bringing all of those feelings and memories back. Her heart was heavy from trying to understand her mother's choice to never come home.

No sooner had they taken seats in the living room than a firm triple knock drew everyone's attention. With butterflies back in full force, Desi started to stand.

Gerda jumped up first. "I'll get it."

Desi sat, crossed one leg over the other and tried to look unfazed but suspected she was doing a horrible job. When Gerda ushered in Kent and Steven, both her aunt and uncle stood to say hello, so she did, too.

There they both were, shower-fresh, dressed for Sunday dinner, Steven looking adorable and Kent looking scrumptious. How was she supposed to ignore Kent with his damp hair curling at his neck?

Once again, Desi hung back, nervous about seeing Kent again, letting her uncle and aunt get first greetings, but finally it couldn't be avoided.

Gerda turned to Desi. "And here's my Desi."

Kent dipped his head in a subtle greeting.

"Hi, Ms. Desi!" Steven shot over to her side as if he hadn't seen her in a month. "I brung these for you." Steven handed her two yellow roses surrounded by Queen Anne's lace. "Look, they match your top."

"Thank you so much." Desi bent to get eye to eye with Steven. Even with her heels on, the boy seemed to grow more every time she saw him, just like the pretty white weeds surrounding her roses. "I'll get a vase." She needed time to gather her nerves and threaten them into submission. No way did she want to let on how anxious she felt being around Kent again.

While she was in the kitchen fussing with the flowers and vase, Gerda breezed in and picked up the tray of appetizers. "Bring the iced tea when you come, please." All business, in her blue top with white lace trim and matching slacks, hair parted in the middle and pulled back into her signature loose bun. Gerda acted more like a caterer than the matriarch of the family, and she made it clear the dinner party had officially begun.

Desi composed herself and got down six glasses, filled five of them with iced tea, deciding to wait to see what Steven wanted, placed them on a tray and brought it into the living room. She handed out the drinks, and when she got to Kent, their eyes met and he didn't look away. It wasn't the iced glasses that gave her a chill.

"Thanks" was all he said, leaving her wondering if he planned to treat her like a stranger all night or the woman he'd kissed as if he'd meant it. So far he was going the *mildly acquainted* route.

She got back to business, handing out drinks. "Steven, would you like apple juice or lemonade?"

"Milk, please. I'm a growing boy."

Gerda laughed. "You certainly are."

As the others enjoyed their drinks and conversation, Gerda grilled the potato pancakes, thin enough to roll each one up, and Desi got the warm serving dish of barley, mushrooms and kale and placed the already-grilled lamb chops in a circle around the top. The rich and rangy aroma of lamb overcame her jittery stomach, and boy, was she ready to eat.

"Put some of that chopped mint on it," Gerda said just before they made their way into the dining room. "Dinner's served."

Without any official seat assignments, Steven rushed to sit next to Desi. She glanced at Kent, who sat directly across from her and next to her aunt at the head of the table. She gave him a hint of a shrug. *I can't help it if your kid loves me. Why'd you accept the invitation if you didn't want him around me?*

Then it dawned on her that maybe *he* was the one who wanted to see her, and Steven was along for the ride. She stopped short of batting her eyes at him to test out her theory.

Other than Kent's stoic silence, dinner conversation flowed easily as plates of food were passed around. She discovered she had the same birthday as one of her cousins, and Erik insisted her voice sounded just like her mother's. A plethora of questions about his long-lost sister followed. Had she ever married? Had she been a talented musician? How in the world had the two of them survived? He mentioned how being five years older, he'd always thought of her as a pest, and he offered regret that they hadn't been closer before he left for college.

Only when Helena put her hand on his arm did he get the picture and forgo his grilling.

Her uncle seemed like a kind man with sympathetic steel-blue eyes, and she wished with all of her heart that her mother hadn't cut off every last family tie. She had a vague memory of Grandma Gerda being at her fifth birthday, and maybe her tenth, but after that she hadn't seen her until her mother was dying.

Though the potato pancake was delicious, it went down like a brown paper bag when the bitter thought struck that maybe her mother had been ashamed of Desi. But her mother had always seemed so proud of her—that couldn't have been the reason for her mother's staying away. Though the meeting was strained at first due to the circumstances, Desi had felt completely accepted by her grandmother from the moment she'd shown up last year in the hospital. It only made sense that their getting reacquainted here in Heartlandia had been a bit tough at first. She'd never felt for one second it was because of her being biracial.

Once she decided to concentrate on the food instead of her insecurity, everything tasted fantastic. Her stomach, however, was still uneasy what with Kent staring at her from across the bountifully filled table. She got the distinct impression he wanted to talk to her.

For distraction, she glanced around as everyone enjoyed their meal. So this was how a family dinner went. Despite her preoccupation with Kent, Desi liked the feel of this gathering. She liked these people, even the aunt and uncle she'd only just met, and the man who'd recently shaken her world with a kiss straight from heaven, but who didn't want to be involved with her. Plus Steven, who currently rested his head on her arm—gosh, he must miss his mommy—and Gerda at the head of the table, the sweet yet stern and endearing grandmother she wished she'd gotten to know better when she'd been a kid.

Desi served Steven another lamb chop and *lefse.* "I miss my mom's cooking," he whispered for only Desi to hear.

She put her arm around him and gathered him to her

side, choosing not to follow Kent's rules because this child needed some lady love. She wanted to tell Steven he could eat with her and Gerda any night he wanted but knew Kent wouldn't like that, so she just squeezed him. Her heart melted for the pining boy, and right now she didn't care if Kent wanted her to back off or not.

"You probably get told you look like Beyoncé all the time, don't you?" Helena asked, a bite of barley halfway to her mouth.

Shocked that anyone would compare her to someone as beautiful as the popular singer, Desi's eyes went wide. "Never, but thank you." Her gaze met Kent's.

His lips twitched in a fleeting smile. "I can see the resemblance."

Not wanting to look away from him, as it was the first time this evening he'd engaged her in any kind of conversation, she paused over his gaze.

"Who's Beyoncé?" No sooner had Gerda asked than Steven filled her in.

Desi didn't want things to get awkward with Kent and shortly switched her line of vision to Helena. "All I can say is, I wish."

After dinner, Uncle Erik and Helena engaged Gerda in a heated conversation about local politics and what she should do as the acting mayor. Desi worried that everyone in town might be doing the same thing, and if so, how could the poor woman please everyone? Before she could fret further, Steven invited her outside.

After a challenging game of three-way Frisbee in the front yard between Desi, Kent and Steven, the boy got engrossed in a handheld video game and they all went back inside. Acting on her earlier hunch that Kent might want to talk to her, Desi sought him out in the living room. He was partially listening to the ongoing conversation between her uncle and grandmother when she appeared, a mug of coffee in each hand.

Her stomach fluttered before she spoke. "Would you like to go out on the porch with me?"

"Sure," he said, rising, immediately rattling Desi, and relieving her of one of the cups.

She sat on the slider love seat. He kept his distance and took the matching wicker chair beside it with the paisley-patterned pillow. Okay, so he didn't want to get close; he'd sent the message loud and clear.

"I owe you an explanation," he said, right off. "I've been bossing you around, telling you to leave my kid alone, and then he practically throws himself at you whenever he sees you. You're probably wondering why."

"You could say that." Since her conversation with her grandmother, she knew about Kent's wife leaving him, but she didn't let on. His earnest expression told her she was about to find out.

"His mother walked out a year ago as if she didn't give a damn about him." He tossed her a steely stare. "It broke his heart." He leaned forward, rested his forearms on his thighs, holding the coffee mug between his hands, and kept his voice down. "I can understand if she wanted to walk out on me, but Steven? I thought I knew her. We were married seven years and had gone steady practically since grammar school."

He stared at his coffee before taking a long drink. Desi took in his comments, sensing something special happening between them. He was opening up to her, like she had the other night with him. But Kent couldn't look more serious if he were pronouncing someone dead. If his wife's leaving had broken Steven's heart, what about Kent's?

"She wanted me to sell the Urgent Care and join this exclusive clinic in San Francisco. Said she was sick of Heartlandia, couldn't live here another day." He glanced up, an incredulous look on his face. "She didn't respect my business or me. I wasn't making enough money. Anyway, I refused to move. Who would want to buy the clinic? And how would Heartlandians get medical care if I shut it down? She gave me an ultimatum, and when I didn't budge, she left. Just like that. Like we didn't mean dirt to her."

Hurt and concern for both Kent and Steven wrapped her like a shawl. She felt compelled to say something, no matter how lame. "I can only imagine…"

"Looking back, I should have seen it coming. And now when I see how Steven's eyes light up every time he sees you, well, it scares me, you know? I can't ever let a woman break his heart like that again."

What about Kent's heart? Would he ever let a woman get close again?

Since Gerda had told her why Kent was so moody and overprotective of his son, she'd had time to think about the situation. And Grandma was right—he *was* scared.

"I can see why you'd feel that way, Kent, but some-times we can't control everything and we have to let life play out and see. Besides, I'm not his mom, just a substitute piano teacher. It's a whole different thing."

"You're a hell of a lot more than that, Desi."

If her tongue wasn't stuck to the roof of her mouth, she'd try to say something. She was a lot more than that? To whom—Kent or Steven? Desi found the sudden need to speed up the sliding rocker but stopped herself. Kent had just blown her mind a second time, and this time it wasn't with a kiss, but words.

Get ahold of yourself. Don't make a big deal out of it. Maybe he only meant she was a hell of a lot more than a substitute piano teacher?

Kent stood and sat next to her, his long arm resting along the top of the love seat behind her. "Don't you realize how much you have to offer?"

Only her mother had ever spoken to her like that—never a man. His words landed like a sucker punch to her solar plexus. She could hardly breathe as her mother's voice sounded clear as ever in her mind. *You have so much to offer the world. Get out there. Stop sticking around for me.* Her mom's prematurely aged face during those last few months before she'd died slammed into her memory and made her cry.

Kent looked horrified.

"I'm sorry. All this talk about mothers leaving got me thinking about my mom." She wiped her nose and sipped her coffee to get a grip.

"I'm here if you want to talk about it. Hell, it's the least I can do after everything I just said."

At first, she didn't want to talk about it, but Kent seemed so genuinely interested, and he had known her mother, even if when only a young boy. She'd had precious few people to tell about everything her mom had gone through. "She suffered so much at the end, fighting to breathe. And the pain. God, nothing was strong enough to stop the pain when that damn lung cancer got into her bones. Sometimes I had to give her so much morphine, I was afraid I'd kill her. Ironic, huh?" She wiped her eyes, embarrassed she'd fallen apart so easily. "I'm sorry."

"Don't be. It hurts me to hear how she suffered, too. Anytime you want to talk about it—" Was this Kent the sensitive man or the doctor talking?

He'd opened up to her about his situation, and now she had an opportunity to share her deepest, darkest feelings. Why not give it a try? Besides, he'd asked for it.

"Sometimes I used to hope that she'd drift away after the morphine. That she wouldn't wake up. Why should she? Why suffer like that? But whenever she was conscious, she looked at me like I was the most wonderful gift in the world, and she'd tell me how she loved me and how much I had to offer. And I loved her so much I never wanted to lose her. Never." She gave an ironic shake of her head. "I was so busy taking care of her, I didn't think about what I wanted to do with my life, let alone what I had to offer. It didn't seem that important."

His arm came off the back of the love seat, settling on her shoulders, rubbing them. The hint of pine and the outdoors came from Kent's aftershave instead of the fresh night air. His touch was tender and warm, and if she wasn't crying, she would have melted into his hold.

"How can I have so much to offer when I don't even know who half of me is? You know?"

She glanced at Kent, thinking how easily they'd opened up to each other. Even his silhouetted profile was gorgeous, and being so close, she couldn't deny for another second that she had a major crush on him. He pulled her toward his chest, and she rested her head on his shoulder. She'd hardly been able to think straight since he'd sprung that amazing kiss on her, and now he was holding her again. It felt snug and heavenly.

But how was she supposed to keep the distance with his son and get closer to Kent at the same time? Besides, she'd been homeschooled by her mother and had never gone on to college. He was a doctor. She and Kent were completely mismatched on so many levels.

The man let his marriage end over refusing to move to San Francisco. He was evidently stubborn and controlling. She'd been a vagabond, yet someone who'd never had the chance to explore life on her own. As soon as she figured out where to find her father, she'd be there in a heartbeat. Finding him was the main reason she'd come back to Oregon. That and spending some time with Gerda. After a while longer here, she planned to move on.

She nestled her head between Kent's neck and shoulder, thinking how strong and comforting he felt and how she could get used to his arms around her. But the timing was way off for any possible relationship. And Kent was right—her leaving wouldn't be fair to Steven, especially since the boy thought so much of her.

Kent ran his hand up and down her arm. "You look really nice tonight."

She smiled, her head still tucked under his chin. "Thank you. You do, too." What could she possibly offer a man like Kent, who was completely out of her league? "Were those flowers from your yard?"

"Yes."

"Were they your idea?"

"Steven's."

Figures. A breathy laugh jerked her shoulders. When she felt his jaw tighten, she assumed he smiled.

After a few more quiet moments, she pulled away and glanced upward. The way he always looked at her with intensity and interest, like right now, and the way he'd kissed her, she knew in her gut their attraction was mutual. She sighed in resignation, knowing that some things, no matter how appealing, were best left alone. What lousy, lousy timing.

"Need a refill on your coffee?" she asked.

"I'm good."

Wanting nothing more than to languish in his embrace for the rest of the night, she went with her better judgment and got up to refill her cup. He'd probably felt the shift in mood, because he followed her inside the house.

"Dad, I beat it! I finally beat the Cyclops kingdom!" Steven waved the hand game like a trophy.

Kent high-fived his son, then thanked Gerda for a fantastic meal and said good-night to Erik and Helena. He glanced at Desi across the room and nodded good-night. Steven was so stoked by his win, he'd forgotten all about her and everyone else and followed his father out the door.

No sooner had the door closed than Steven burst back through, running straight for Desi. He hugged her around the waist. "I forgot to say goodbye!"

Next he hugged Gerda. "Thanks. I'm stuffed."

Then off he sprang for home, leaving Desi laughing and filled with genuine affection for the kid. And his father.

Thursday morning, Grandma acted strange. She hadn't touched her breakfast, and her ritual cup of tea sat cold on the table. She'd had another one of those special meetings Wednesday night, had come home after ten and gone straight to bed. She sat at the kitchen table in her bathrobe, hand across her mouth, staring out the window. "Look at that covey of quail," she muttered. "They're finally using that feeder I set out."

Desi gazed out the window and found the gray-and-black birds with the stylish feather hats pecking around the feeder. "Do you want me to make you another cup of tea?"

"What?" Gerda said, as if startled out of deep thought.

"More tea?" Desi pointed to her cup. Gerda glanced at it as if she'd forgotten what tea was, then shook her head. "Are you okay?"

She took a long inhalation. "I've got a lot on my mind, that's all."

Not able to pry anything else out of her grandmother, Desi went about her chores and the last of her current calligraphy job. Two years back, she'd agreed to do wedding invitations for the daughter of one of her mother's musician friends. Everyone loved them, and several of the daughter's friends had asked Desi to do their invitations, too. This was the latest and biggest job yet.

Tonight for dessert, as a thank-you for the wonderful Sunday dinner, she decided to surprise Grandma with the one Scandinavian dish her mother had taught her to make, *krumkake*. It was something like a waffle cookie, and she'd need fresh eggs and real cream to make sure they came out perfect.

When Gerda was still sequestered in her bedroom, Desi decided to borrow the car and go to the post office to mail off the completed invitations, then she'd go on to the market. Before she left, she grabbed Gerda's grocery list from the notepad on the refrigerator and headed out the door. It was almost lunchtime and she wanted to be back in time to make lunch for her grandmother and to give herself plenty of time to prepare for that afternoon's piano lessons. She allowed herself only one glance next door to Kent's house on the walk to the car. With Steven at summer day camp and Kent at the Urgent Care, it looked quiet.

For Tuesday's piano lesson, the babysitter had brought and picked Steven up, saving Desi the difficult task of facing Kent after she'd made up her mind to leave him alone. He hadn't come around their house, either, so they'd probably both come to the same conclusion. Some things were best left unexplored. In this case, it was the wisest thing to do.

Desi got home a little later than she'd meant to, and she found Gerda downstairs in her den on the phone, with no less than three notepads for reference in front of her. She hadn't bothered to put her hair in a bun today, and there was no evidence of her having yet eaten lunch.

"I'm heating some soup. Want some?" Desi asked once Gerda had hung up the phone.

"No, thank you, dear. Could you bring me some antacid?"

Desi found the bright pink medicine and headed for the den. "Aren't you feeling well?"

"Nervous stomach is all." Gerda offered a wan smile and gratefully accepted the bottle.

Four hours later, after three piano students and still no sign of Gerda leaving her makeshift office, Desi fixed a simple dinner from leftovers. She'd had a fun and messy baking session and wanted to make sure they saved room for dessert.

Gerda tried to be polite and eat, but she only picked at her food. She really didn't seem to have an appetite, so why force her to eat dessert? Maybe tonight wasn't such a great time to spring the *krumkake* on her. It could keep.

"I'm worried about you, Grandma."

"Oh, it's nothing. Nothing at all." Gerda pushed her plate away and tugged on the stringy fringe of the place mat. "Just a lot of silly city business on my mind." She stood, looking less straight and more fragile. "I think I'll read in my room for a while."

Worry trickled over Desi as she watched her grandmother amble off. What if the woman was sick and not telling her? What if Desi lost her after only just getting to know her? Old anxieties nearly swept Desi away, but she talked herself down. Gerda was fine, just preoccupied with her city council. Knowing Heartlandia meant the world to her grandmother, she figured something big must be going on. That was all it was, and from the way it was tearing up her grandmother, that was more than enough.

A surprising tender feeling for Gerda made Desi pause while washing the dinner dishes. How quickly she'd grown to genuinely care for the woman, how at home she'd felt the past two and a half weeks, and how much Gerda's withdrawing made Desi worry.

As she put the dishes away, her mind drifted to Heartlandia, her mother's home and the town her mother had run away from. It was the place that had shaped her mom as much as Gerda and Edvard Rask had.

There was so little she knew about her mother's early years, and letting Grandma remain withdrawn and distracted by city business couldn't be good for her. Desi made a snap decision to heat some water for tea and carry a plate of the *krumkake* up to Gerda's room. Truth was, she was lonely and filled with questions and finally felt ready to broach the questions to which only her grandmother knew the answers.

A few minutes later, armed with dessert on a tray, she tapped on Gerda's bedroom door.

"Come in." Her voice sounded aged and weak.

Gerda was still dressed, and she sat in an overstuffed lounger beside her bed, reading several pages from a typed letter.

"I brought some goodies, and I won't take no for an answer."

Gerda's eyes brightened when she saw the *krumkake.*

"Momma taught me how to make this. We'd have it on special occasions." Gerda's wrinkled smile warmed Desi's insides. "I made them especially for you."

"Then I will have one. To be honest, I am hungry. It's just my stomach is all knotted up."

"What's going on over there at city hall to make you so upset?"

"They promised I'd just be a figurehead when I agreed to fill in, but I can't sit back and smile about everything."

"Trouble?"

"I'm not at liberty to talk." Her index finger shot up. "Oh, though I do have a question for you. Will you teach me how to open and reply to emails? The secretary types up all of the notes from our meetings and emails them to everyone. I'm the only one she can't send them to, and I'm supposed to be the mayor." She waved the loose pages as evidence.

"Of course I can help you with that. And I have a special request for you, too." Desi poured the tea and handed her grandmother a *krumkake* with powdered sugar on top. "I have so many questions about my mother and her growing up here. Can you share some of your memories with me?"

Gerda's hand went to her heart. "Oh, my goodness, I'd love to. I should have shared with you sooner, but..."

"But I didn't ask until now."

"Yes." Gerda smiled and reached out for a hug from Desi. "I'm glad you did."

"Let's eat our *krumkake* first."

"Good plan."

Desi ate in hungry silence, and the dessert tasted just as good as it always had, but Gerda took only a few bites.

"Not good?" Desi asked.

"Delicious. It's just my nervous stomach."

Was it all city hall that made Grandma nervous, or was Desi adding to it by probing into the past?

Gerda took one more bite, then put her plate on the bedside table. "Now, you'll have to help me get the box down where I keep all of her yearbooks and special school things."

After she'd finished her tea and Desi licked every last remnant of powdered sugar from her fingertips, she followed her grandmother down the hall to an out-of-the-way closet.

"Your mother was very temperamental, like her father, and I'm ashamed to report we fought a lot. If I said red she'd say blue. Used to drive Edvard crazy. Maybe I was too protective of her, but I just wanted the best."

Desi pulled a chain and a dim lightbulb offered a glimpse of several stacked boxes, some marked with Ester's name. Way in the back was one with "High School" written in black permanent marker.

"Let's start with that one," Gerda said, "and we can work our way back from there."

Desi retrieved the box and hoisted it onto her shoulder, then they started back down the hall to her grandmother's bedroom.

"When your mother was a little tot, she used to run down this hall every morning and jump onto the bed with Edvard and me. She was an early bird, that one was, better than an alarm clock."

Desi heard the affection in Gerda's voice and tried to imagine her mother as a little girl.

"She had the most beautiful white-blond hair, and her eyes were brighter than the sun. I'd snuggle her close between her daddy and me, and it felt perfect." Gerda's step faltered. Desi backed up and put her arm around her waist and walked her back to the bedroom, worrying that maybe all the memories might be too much for her grandmother.

"Your grandfather was hard to please and very old-fashioned. Your mother ran away rather than tell him she was pregnant." She shook her head as if all the horrible memories had come rushing back. "The whole town had been looking for her when she'd gone missing, and months later when we found out she was in the hospital in St. Louis, Edvard and I flew out to bring her home."

Now tears formed in Gerda's eyes, washing over the look that could only be described as *regret*. "She'd just given birth to you." Gerda took and squeezed Desi's free hand. "Edvard was so old-fashioned. He was upset, and Ester told him to get out of her life." She shook her head. "What could I do?"

A moment passed as Gerda drew herself together.

"Ester let me hold you." A tiny smile creased her wrinkled lips. "What should I have done, Desi? Go with my husband or stay with my daughter and grandchild?"

Desi's chest grew tight with emotion—love, hurt, anger, sadness—as she put the box on the bed and took her grandmother into her arms and held on tight.

Mother had taught her when a woman entered into a relationship with a man it should always be on equal footing, but grandmother's generation hadn't necessarily gotten that message.

Now Gerda wept. "We came home and told everyone we'd found our Ester, that she was fine and had a job in Missouri, and Edvard never spoke about her again."

"But, Grandma, I feel like I remember you at a couple of my birthdays."

She nodded her head on Desi's shoulder. "Yes. I begged Edvard to come with me, but he was so stubborn, and your mother was just as bad, saying she never wanted to see him again, either. I came for your fifth and tenth birthdays. But when you turned fifteen, well, Edvard had gotten sick and I couldn't leave him alone."

"I wish I could have known you better."

"Me, too. You have no idea." Gerda squeezed Desi's shoulders.

After a long hug, Gerda sat down on her bedside lounger. As if stalling, she took another bite of her half-finished dessert. "Hmm, this really is delicious. I couldn't make them any better myself."

Having her grandmother's approval meant the world to Desi, and she knew her mother would be proud. Gerda and Desi shared a heartfelt smile. The truth had finally come out—her grandfather hadn't been able to accept a biracial baby—and now they were about to embark on a very special journey together. "Shall we?" Desi reached for the box lid.

Something about the pyramid of creases on her grandmother's forehead gave Desi pause. Waltzing down memory lane wouldn't be easy for either of them.

"Once, Ester wanted to go to a concert in Portland. Edvard put his foot down and said no. We thought she'd taken it pretty well, until the night of the concert, when she climbed out her window and snuck out to go anyway."

Desi's hand flew to her mouth. *From the second floor?* Hearing about this other side of her mother made her wonder how many other things she'd never shared. "What did you do?" Desi wiped away some dust from the box on the bedspread and sat.

"We didn't even realize she'd gone until we heard someone coming through the front door at one in the morning." Gerda's hand went to her cheek. "I thought Edvard would have a stroke right then and there. Her brother had never given us trouble. She was only sixteen!"

Her mother had never talked much about high school. Or anything else. Desi wished with all of her heart she could ask her how her life had been growing up. She glanced at Gerda, who was looking pale and withdrawn. She'd just admitted her husband had been ashamed of his daughter having a baby out of wedlock—a baby of color, no less—and she'd stayed by his side until his death. Was the pained expression regret?

Because that was exactly how Desi felt. How would everyone's lives have been if Edvard had reacted differently?

Desi refocused in order to drop the negative feelings

for her grandfather and opened the box then lifted out several school annuals. "Which one first?"

Gerda checked out the years and chose the bright red yearbook. "This one is from Ester's senior year. Let's start with this one."

Desi snuggled next to Gerda on the lounger, where the light was best, and opened the book to the first page.

"Your mother was involved in everything—cheer-leading, music, drama, even the school newspaper. Oh, look, here's her senior picture."

Desi first glanced at her grandmother, whose eyes welled with moisture again, then at the typical senior portrait of a beautiful girl with clear blue eyes and straight blond hair. There was confidence in her smile and maybe a hint of mischief in her expression. Desi remembered seeing that spirited look whenever her mother felt challenged.

Gerda turned the page. "Oh, and look at that pose." She laughed. "Ester took cheerleading very seriously. Nearly broke her arm once doing that silly human-pyramid thing."

Desi smiled with pride at the picture of her mother holding pom-poms in the air while doing a split. She could practically hear her call out *Go, fight, win!*

It occurred to Desi that her mother had only rarely talked about her cheerleading. Desi had always thought it was because she was homeschooling her, and a home-schooled girl couldn't exactly be involved in a school sports program. Not when they moved around so much, anyway.

"She was all set to go off to college that summer... then she was gone." Gerda's hand went to her chest again; she clutched her blouse. "Oh, dear. Oh, dear."

"Is this too much for you, Grandma?"

"Oh!" Her pained expression sent a chill through Desi.

"Are you okay?"

Gerda held her breath for a second, then let up on the death clutch to her blouse. "I got a sharp gas pain, that's all. It's better now."

Leery of her excuse, Desi watched and worried. "Maybe a sip of tea will help?"

"That would be good."

Desi poured her more tea. Gerda reached for the tea-cup and took a sip, quickly putting the cup down and grabbing her chest again. "Oh!"

Chapter Six

Desi sat in the waiting room of the Urgent Care after the nurse whisked Gerda in to be examined. She'd wanted to go in with her grandmother, but Gerda had waved her off, and the no-nonsense silver-haired nurse didn't seem too thrilled about the possibility of Desi getting in the way, either.

"I'll be fine," Gerda said. "Kent will take care of me."

Knowing that Kent would be in charge helped a little, but her nerves were still ruling the day. There she sat on a hard bench, wringing her hands in her lap, worried sick. She'd felt this way before—every time her mother had needed to be rushed to the hospital. She'd never get used to it. Hated it.

The clinic was typical with sterile gray walls and subtle printed linoleum floors. The only decorations were some fake ficus trees in large colorful pots. Nurses bustled in and out of rooms, calling out requests or giving directions to each other. The term *controlled chaos* came to mind, and she'd seen it all before. This was the way the medical system worked. There was no way to predict on any given day or hour how many patients would show up for care.

The waiting room had been packed when they'd arrived, but the instant Desi had mentioned chest pain, they were brought straight in.

A half hour later, Desi was on her way back from making a bathroom stop when the silver-haired nurse who'd taken Gerda away stopped her in the hall.

"Would you like to see your grandmother?"

"Yes. Is she all right?"

"She's fine and in the procedure room. Follow me."

Desi found Kent standing beside Gerda's gurney, talking quietly to her and writing on his prescription pad. He looked casual but entirely in control and in total concentration, with one foot propped on a stool, his powerful shoulders sloped just enough to write with the pad balancing on his thigh.

"Hi, Grandma. How do you feel?"

All of the worry lines Gerda had worn into the Urgent Care had smoothed. She smiled at Desi. "I'm fine. It wasn't my heart after all, as it turns out."

Kent turned and found Desi's questioning gaze. "Hey," he said. His greeting sounded anything but professional.

"What's the word?" she asked.

"Your grandmother is suffering from stress. We did an EKG, which was fine, and some blood tests. Though it will take a few hours for all of them to come back, the initial cardiac enzyme test looks good. But Gerda's vital signs are elevated."

"I never have high blood pressure," Gerda broke in.

"Except for today," Kent replied.

Gerda nodded in agreement. Kent glanced at Desi as if making a point that it also wasn't every day a long-lost granddaughter worked her way back into her life.

Point taken.

Kent looked like a TV doctor in his white jacket with a stethoscope hanging around his neck. He tore off a tiny paper from his pad and handed it to Gerda. "I'm sending you home with a better antacid than that over-the-counter stuff and some sedatives. I want you to take one of both as soon as you get home, and for the next couple of days keep taking the sedative until you relax and your blood pressure is back to normal. I'll write out the instructions." He shifted his attention from Gerda to Desi. "Make sure she doesn't exert herself for a couple of days. No mayor duties. And no driving." He looked back to Gerda. "Did you hear me? Don't exert yourself, okay?"

"I'm old, Kent, but I'm not hard of hearing."

He gave an exaggerated nod. "This is true."

Sure, he'd known Gerda all his life, but his bedside manner was easygoing and reassuring, and Desi would bet her classic-jazz record collection that he was like that with all of his patients.

"We're going to wait until the IV finishes before we let her go home. On top of everything else, she was a little dehydrated."

"Makes sense since she didn't eat and hardly drank all day."

Kent took the prescription back from Gerda and handed it to Desi. "You may want to fill this while you're waiting, to speed things up." He walked with her and guided her out the door.

"I'll be right back, Grandma," Desi said, relieved that her grandmother was okay, but completely aware of the warm pressure from Kent's hold on her arm.

He stopped just outside the examination room, out of Gerda's line of vision. "She's totally upset about something, and it has driven her blood pressure way up. She needs to relax or she might develop palpitations."

"I'll make sure she calms down."

"Anything going on between you two?"

"Us? No. We're good. We were looking at some of my mother's things earlier, and…"

"This condition doesn't strike me as anything that came on suddenly."

"No. She's been preoccupied with some meetings at city hall, but that's all."

"Well, make sure she relaxes for the next few days."

"Will do, Doc."

They walked the long clinic corridor, which was cluttered with stray equipment and metal tables. This place didn't quite have the medicinal smell of a hospital, but it came close.

"The pharmacy's just across the street. Shouldn't take more than fifteen minutes to fill it, and I promise we'll have Gerda out of here within the half hour."

"I can't thank you enough."

"This is what I do, you know. It's my job."

"Right. I know, but I mean, I'm just glad it wasn't her heart, and I'm glad you were the one to tell her." *And to take care of her.*

"No problem there. Her EKG was fine."

"And I'm glad you didn't move to San Francisco and sell this clinic."

He sent her a thoughtful glance, hopefully taking her comments as they were meant: a compliment.

"Dr. Larson?" A tall, thin nurse rushed toward him with a handful of paperwork. "We've got a patient with severe abdominal pain in room ten."

Kent took the sheets of paper. "I'll be right there." He turned back to Desi and took her hand, gave it a quick squeeze then let go. "This is a crazy place to meet up, but it was good to see you again." His gaze did a quick survey of her, head to toe. She hoped he didn't do that with all of his patients or family members. Something about that sexy gaze told her he didn't. "Don't hesitate to call if you need me." And he was off.

Basking in the sweet and warm sensations enveloping her, she watched him stride down the hall, larger-than-life, confident and professional as all hell. Wow. Grandma was in excellent hands. She rubbed where he'd held her arm then turned and headed for the pharmacy, fingers crossed she might see Kent one more time before she took her grandmother home.

While waiting for the medicine, it occurred to Desi how important her grandmother had become. Gerda had opened her home and arms the instant Desi had mentioned she'd wanted to come to Heartlandia. As if she'd been waiting all of Desi's life to have her there. She'd been kind and encouraging ever since Desi had arrived, and Desi felt something more from Grandma, too. She felt loved. Unconditionally.

Desi blinked back the sudden rush of moisture in her eyes, realizing she loved her grandmother, too. Now that they'd been through an emergency together, they were true family.

With a heart filled with a sense of belonging—something she'd missed since her mother had died—Desi retrieved the medicine when her grandmother's name was called. She smiled all the way back to the Urgent Care, ready to take her long-lost grammy home.

Two hours later, Desi had tucked Gerda into bed. It was eleven o'clock. Her silver-and-white hair lay thinly over her shoulders on top of an old-fashioned nightgown, complete with lace trim along the neck and shoulders. The sedative made her softly etched skin look saggy, and her normal healthy glow dimmed. She seemed vulnerable and Desi worried about her. What could be eating at her enough to cause chest pain?

A sudden urge made Desi crawl onto the bed beside her and lie on top of the blanket to cuddle near her grandmother. "Mind if I stay with you for a while, Grandma? Just until you fall asleep?"

Gerda smiled and welcomed her with open arms. "I'd love it."

They snuggled in silence for a few moments, lights on, old-house noises creaking and cracking around them. Desi detected the clean scent of cold cream and loved how at home she felt.

Gerda inhaled long and slow. "I've got a lot on my mind these days, and it feels like this huge weight on my chest."

"I hope it's not because of me."

"No. No. You're the best part these days."

"Sometimes it helps to share worries."

Gerda played with and patted Desi's hair. Desi glanced up at her face.

"But I've been sworn to silence." She bit her lip, knitting her fair brows. "There's something crazy happening in our town, and I'm half-sick about it."

Desi sat up. "This is the most peaceful and ideal town I've ever been in. What could possibly change that? Zombies?" she teased. "Are there werewolves roaming the pine forest?"

Gerda huffed and rolled her dull blue eyes. "You wouldn't believe it if I told you."

She had Desi's full curiosity. "Want to try me?"

Gerda sat up and smoothed the creases in the sheets. "I'm not supposed to talk about it to anyone outside of the city council. I gave them my word."

"And your word nearly had you admitted to the hospital tonight. Sometimes sharing a burden makes it lighter."

"I feel like they set me up. Made it sound so easy to step in as mayor. 'Just until we can have an election,' they said. 'You'll only be a figurehead.' Now I feel set up, like they were saving this for—how do they say it on TV?—for my watch."

A battle ensued inside Gerda, and her conflicted expression made Desi understand the importance of Grandma's word. If she said she'd keep a secret, well, she'd keep it even if it made her sick.

"All the more reason to share."

"Oh, Desi, I..."

Feeling guilty for putting more pressure on her grandmother, Desi backed off. "You don't have to tell me, Grandma. I understand. You made a promise."

Another deep breath lifted Gerda's chest. "The thing

is—I want to. I know I can trust you, and no one will ever find out, will they?"

"You have my solemn vow." Desi raised her right hand and made her most trustworthy face, then crossed her heart for good measure.

Gerda laughed. "That's exactly what I said my first day on the job as mayor."

They chuckled together, holding hands and smiling at each other, enjoying the few lighter moments.

Gerda made a playful expression. "This sedative is making me feel all swimmy-headed and a little loose-lipped."

Desi winked. "You do look awfully relaxed." She didn't think she could feel any fonder of her grandmother at that moment.

"Secrets are hard to keep when you feel all loosey-goosey."

Desi kept grinning, sensing the vault was about to crack. She lay back down beside Gerda, so as not to stare at her. Gerda grabbed her hand and squeezed.

"Heartlandia doesn't have a lot of natural resources anymore. The fishing industry has moved north and we aren't rich in anything but trees, and we want to keep them, not cut them down. What small textile factories we once had have all closed over the last twenty years or so.

"A hundred years ago, our astute mayor Bjarnesen set out to make us the best little tourist town in Oregon. He opened our port to cruise ships, made sure the trains took extra-long stops here and campaigned for better roads and highways out this way. More and more families turned their big old houses into bed-and-breakfasts or rentals. Everyone took extra-good care of their property and homes. The town focused on all the things that would bring people here for vacations. Novelty shops, Scandinavian goods, excellent yet inexpensive restaurants. The mayor even built the Heritage Theater and brought in talented musicians and singers from all over the country."

Gerda took a sip of the water from the glass on the bedside table that Desi had left for her. "This medicine makes my mouth dry." She took another sip and wiped a drop that slipped out. "He put us on the map and we've been living a modest but contented life as a tourist attraction ever since. We've built our reputation as a place where people work together for a better life. Fishermen and Native Americans, Scandinavian and American. Heartlandians. We boast how the Chinook people nursed shipwrecked sailors back to health and taught them the secrets of hunting and fishing our oftentimes-treacherous river waters."

Gerda yawned and cast a quick glance Desi's way, finding her undivided attention, then laid her head back on her pillow.

"You probably haven't been there yet, but we have a two-mile-long brick wall called the Ringmiren that the first Scandinavian settlers helped the Chinook people build. It circles the farthest limits of our city and it delineates the sacred Chinook burial ground. It's said that thousands of souls lie in rest there, and it is a sacred place."

"I didn't know any of this, Grandma. It's fascinating. Will you take me there?"

Gerda nodded, looking very sleepy. "It took ten years of preparation, and two years to build, but last year we finally finished our own city college." Her voice grew weaker. "I chaired the board for the city-college project. We thought it would bring more opportunity for employment for residents and also draw students from surrounding cities to attend. We hired our wealthiest businessman and contractor, Leif Andersen, to build the college from our designs, and it is beautiful, too. He did a fantastic job." Gerda lifted her head again and took another drink of water, and Desi thought soon she'd need to refill the glass.

Worry changed her expression. "During the process of building, Leif's construction crew dug up some old trunks filled with antique sea navigation instruments and a captain's journals."

Desi had been enthralled before, but the new twist riveted her attention. "Are you serious? Wow."

Gerda wiped her brow, pushing a few errant strands of hair aside. "'Wow' is right." Her eyes blinked open and closed as if she fought off sleep. "We've brought in a history expert who teaches at the college, Elke Norling. She's the sister of one of our police sergeants who's on this special council with me. You met him at the festival. Kent's friend Gunnar?"

Desi nodded, remembering the solidly built police officer with flashing green eyes and a cautious demeanor.

Gerda yawned again. "Anyway, as you can imagine, we've been going through these journals with a fine-tooth comb and they tell an earlier and very different history for our town."

"What do you mean?"

"We've just scratched the surface, but if we can authenticate these journals, which is what we're working on, we will have to face the fact that our beautiful little history of Heartlandia is only partly true. And the big question is what we should do about it."

"But isn't it better to know the whole story? The complete history?"

"Not when our livelihood depends on our selling ourselves as a peaceful storybook town catering to tourists." Gerda sought out Desi's eyes and held her gaze. "Not when these captain's journals tell dark, dismal horror stories about our past. Not when we have to face up to the possibility that Hjartalanda was discovered by a scurrilous ship captain. A pirate." She'd spit out the word as if it had tasted horrible.

Desi's mouth dropped. "A pirate?"

Gerda, who looked more and more haggard as she unwound her tale, nodded. "A pirate."

Chapter Seven

Desi watched her grandmother drift off to sleep just after getting to the meaty part of her tale. Amazing. A pirate had first discovered Heartlandia. Captain Jack Sparrow, perhaps? Desi snickered and fought the urge to wake her grandmother to get the rest of the story out of her, but instead she gently covered her to her chin, then turned off the light and tiptoed out of the room.

No wonder the acting mayor of perfect little Heartlandia was having chest pain.

How in the world was Desi supposed to process this crazy information? Of course she would keep it to herself as she'd promised, but, wow, what a wickedly fun twist for a town known as paradise.

She went downstairs to shut off the rest of the lights and made sure the front door was locked. Just before she turned off the dining room light, she saw Kent's truck pull to the curb. It was half past midnight.

Guiltily she stood like a voyeur and watched his tall yet graceful frame exit the car and smoothly stride to his front door, the walk of a confident man who'd worked hard and done a lot of good for his community that night. There was much to like and respect about him. The fact that he was gorgeous was icing on the cake.

She allowed herself to entertain a quick fantasy about how it would feel to be waiting up for him and fall into his arms as soon as he came through the door. She'd never waited up for any man. Clicking back into reality, she made a right turn and walked toward the dining room switch plate. No point in dreaming about something that would never happen.

A quiet tapping on the front door snagged her attention before she reached her mark. Making her way back to the door, she looked through the peephole. It was too dark to see anything but a shadow.

"Desi?"

Her pulse nearly leaped in her chest. "Kent?" Hadn't she just watched him head for his house? With leftover habits from L.A., she left the chain latched and opened the door, first making sure it really *was* Kent. "Hey," she said through the crack. With nervous fingers she quickly unlatched the chain and opened the door wider.

"How's she doing?" His huge and sturdy silhouette loomed so near, she fought the urge to run her hands across his chest to make sure he wasn't a ghost.

"She's asleep now. Doing well." Seeing him in the dark sent all kinds of reactions buzzing through her body.

The white of his teeth as he smiled made a chill bubble burst in her chest and ripple across her shoulders. "Good. Don't let her—"

"Exert herself," she finished for him, returning his grin. "I won't." For the second time that night she raised her hand in an oath. "I promise."

He lingered, taunting her with his gorgeousness. "Good. I'll check back tomorrow."

On the verge of saying the requisite "You don't have to," she stopped herself. Even though she had things under control, she didn't want to ruin her chance of seeing him again. "Thanks."

They stood watching each other for a few more heartbeats. Desi felt kind of goofy, and her cheeks were on the verge of cramping from all the grinning, but she did not want to be the first to say good-night and close the door. This crush really did have to stop.

He nodded, uncomfortably. "Well, I better let my sitter go. Good night."

"Good night." She still couldn't bring herself to close the door, and instead she stood like a silly teenager, smitten with the mysterious man next door, watching him walk away.

With Kent the last person she'd see for the night, she predicted she'd have extra sweet, and sexy, dreams.

The next morning Desi helped Gerda brush her hair and twist it into a bun.

"How do people take medicine all the time?" Gerda said. "All I want to do is sleep."

"That's why it's called a sedative, Grandma. And you're not supposed to live on them, only take them when you need to. Like now."

Gerda reached behind for Desi's forearm and squeezed.

"I love it when you call me Grandma." She wasn't sure when the term had entered her vocabulary, but now that Gerda had pointed it out, it did feel good.

Desi bent forward and hugged her around the shoulders. "Ready for breakfast?"

Making sure Gerda was steady enough on her feet to take the stairs down to the kitchen, Desi held her by the waist and hand. "Oatmeal? Eggs? What's it going to be?"

"How about some tea and toast."

"Ah, the breakfast of champions, I see." Not a very hardy way to start the day, but considering Gerda had barely eaten at all yesterday, this was progress, and Desi wasn't about to push the point.

Zipping around the kitchen in old stretched-out sweats and a hoodie, Desi made them both breakfast then washed the dishes and set up Gerda in the screened back porch, the room Gerda called the sunroom, to rest and read some magazines. She opted not to bring up the mind-blowing topic of conversation from last night, wondering if Gerda even remembered it. Maybe she thought she'd dreamed it, but one thing was sure: this morning Gerda hadn't uttered another word about the role of Captain Jack in Heartlandia.

Finally ready to head upstairs to shower, Desi hustled toward the living room, her hand on the banister, ready to swing around the bend, when the doorbell rang. She checked the grandfather clock across the entryway. It was only eight-fifteen. With her hair a straggly mess, feet bare, and wearing seriously old gray sweats, she swung the door open.

There stood Kent, fresh as a cover model, in a pale blue tailored button-down shirt, patterned tie and navy slacks that fit those narrow hips perfectly. She wanted to purr and scream at the same time. She gulped instead. "Hi!"

"Hey. Just dropped Steven off at summer day camp and thought I'd check on Gerda before I head off to the clinic."

She also wanted to run for cover, pull the hood over her head and hunch over so he couldn't see her unwashed face. But she did the right thing and led him down the hall to the sunny porch.

Gerda's expression brightened the instant Kent stepped outside. Whose wouldn't? The guy was a dream machine with that square jaw and naturally hooded set of bedroom eyes.

"How're you doing today?" He went directly to Gerda, pulling out his stethoscope and a small machine from his briefcase.

"Is this a house call? For me?"

"Just checking up on my favorite neighbor."

Gerda smiled and let him listen to her heart then take her blood pressure.

"Much better. One-thirty over eighty-five."

"I'm usually less than that."

Desi enjoyed the view of his back and broad shoulders as he leaned over Gerda. The view of his backside in those perfectly fitted slacks nearly made Desi's mouth drop.

"We're working our way down, but keep taking the sedative today. Be sure to eat and drink lots of fluids. Okay?" He stood up, affording Desi the vision of those amazing buns at work. "I'll check in again when I get home today."

He turned and smiled at Desi, and comparing his

gorgeousness with her morning frumpiness, she wanted to dissolve into the antique braided oval rug.

"Take good care of her."

"She has been," Gerda broke in. "I'm getting spoiled."

"Thanks, Grandma."

"When I was a kid and got sick, Gerda always brought over homemade soup." Kent smiled at his patient, then looked toward Desi, making her bare toes curl with embarrassment.

"You were such a healthy kid, I always worried when you actually got sick."

"That's exactly how I feel about you, Gerda. Hey, I know a chef who makes great chicken gumbo soup. I'll bring some by for your dinner. How's that?"

"My mother always taught me to never argue with a handsome man." Gerda's candid reply made Desi know for a fact the morning's sedative had kicked in.

Kent actually seemed flustered, as if he wasn't prepared to hear that from Gerda. He must have been told how good-looking he was, probably by gazillions of women, but maybe never from a seventysomething matriarch of Heartlandia before. Hey, the woman might be under stress, but she was far from dead.

Hard to believe he didn't have a clue about his effect on women.

Desi smiled inside as she let Kent see himself out. She'd endured enough humiliation over her appearance today. Why add another fifteen or twenty seconds walking him to the door? Instead, she stood at the sunroom entrance and followed him with her stare, a straight shot down the hall. There really was something special about a man whose good looks hadn't gone to his head.

Desi scrubbed her face with her hands. What the heck

was she doing letting her crush get bigger? It couldn't turn into anything. Neither of them was in the right place, and who was she to think he'd give her the time of day if she proclaimed her crush anyway?

Well, there was that amazing kiss…that *he'd* instigated…

This line of thinking was entirely too heavy for eight-thirty in the morning, and she barreled up the stairs to shower and dress. No way would Kent find her a mess when he returned with dinner tonight.

Back with dinner as he'd promised, Kent showed up at six-thirty. Only problem was, taking care of a sedated Gerda had been a really huge job. Along with canceling all of her mayoral appointments for the day, Desi had cleared her calendar for Monday, too.

Desi had wound up taking a second shower when she'd helped her grandmother bathe. During lunch she'd managed to spill more than eat. Desi had to spoon-feed her tea that afternoon since she could barely keep her eyes open.

Maybe it was time to cut her off those sedatives.

When Desi opened the door for Kent, he held a large carton that smelled heavenly. She knew she looked frazzled and her hair was askew with tiny curls overpowering waves, and she'd forgotten to put a speck of makeup on. What a mess.

He smiled anyway. "Cliff Lincoln said to say hello. He made a special batch of chicken gumbo for Gerda, too."

Desi reminded herself what a small town Heartlandia was. "Thanks. You staying?"

"Nope. Friday night is pizza-and-video night with Steven. *Transformers* awaits."

"Well, it certainly was sweet of you to look after Gerda like this."

"She's been the one solid person in my life during all its changes. First my sister moved away from home. Then my parents moved to Bend." He got sullen as he handed her the bag of food, but only briefly. "And you know the rest of the story. Anyway, through it all your grandmother was always there for me. This is the least I can do."

"It smells great. I'll be sure to let Cliff know how much we enjoyed it."

"He threw in some of his cheddar cheese biscuits and fried okra, too." Kent cracked a smile that nearly made Desi drop the soup. "He said the okra was for you."

She sputtered a laugh, getting the inside joke. Cliff was a big tease, but awfully sweet. "He knows I'm out of touch on the soul-food train."

Her mouth watered, but not for the okra. There was that smile lingering on those handsomely formed lips. Right now she imagined what it would be like to kiss Kent Larson again. The thought ran through her body like warm gumbo sliding down the throat.

A pizza truck pulled to the curb in front of Kent's house.

"Gotta go," he said, breaking the lingering look, rushing down the porch steps and across the yard.

Saturday morning, again before nine, Kent showed up on the doorstep. This time Desi was ready for him. She'd gotten up extra early, showered and put on her newest jeans and favorite red top. She was barefoot

again but had given herself a pedicure after putting
Gerda to bed last night. She'd also spent plenty of time
with her trusty curling iron to make sure her hair was
styled into submission.

She opened the door with a flourish, the way she
imagined Clair Huxtable might. Yes, she'd watched *The
Cosby Show* reruns while polishing her toes last night.
When she was a kid she used to pretend she was part
of their family. "Hi!" She smiled with all of her heart,
knowing her red lip gloss sparkled.

She immediately noticed his favorable response, the
glint in his eyes and the slow and thorough scan from
her toes up to her head. Oh, yeah, he liked what he
saw. "Hey."

Unlike his usual, he wore casual clothes—gray ath-
letic shorts, loose white T-shirt and sports trainers—
and he looked fit and fantastic with muscular legs and
arms lightly dusted in blond hair.

"She's in the kitchen. Come in." Desi turned and took
off, knowing how perfectly her jeans fit and giving Kent
some of his own medicine. And yes, she wasn't above
exaggerating her walk. Just a little.

Kent pulled his stethoscope and the small automatic
blood-pressure monitor from his backpack and did his
thing again. Desi looked on, noticing his long fingers
and the size of his palms. The guy was a giant. Yet he
couldn't have been gentler with her grandmother.

"You can cut back on the sedatives today. Just take
half a dose. Then tomorrow, if your blood pressure is
still normal, I'll let you stop taking them altogether."

"I like your plan, my good man," Gerda said. Desi
had gotten used to her grandmother being more loose-
lipped the past two days, but Kent's amused expression

reminded her this was a different Gerda Rask. "By the way, that was the most delicious soup."

"She had two bowls," Desi said. "I nearly had to fight her to get my share."

"That's great. So your stomach is doing better, too, huh?"

Gerda nodded. "I got a lot off my chest the other night. My stomach is better for it."

Desi knew exactly what Gerda referred to. They hadn't broached the subject of her mother or grandfather, or pirates and city-council promises since Thursday night. Still, she was glad to have helped relieve some of the stress by being a good listener when her grandmother needed her.

"Okay, but you still need to take the stomach meds until it runs out. Gastritis takes a while to heal."

"Aye, aye, captain." Gerda snickered.

Oh, yeah, she remembered their talk.

As Desi walked with Kent to the door, besides thinking what a good man he was, she treated herself to a second long look at his muscular legs and well-developed calves. She could only imagine what the rest of him looked like. A thorough vision sprang up and the thought sent a hot rush to her face. She'd let her imagination take her too far.

"Where're you headed?" she asked, quickly getting her breathing under control.

"Steven's in a basketball league. He's got two games today." The more Desi found out about Kent, the more she liked. He was a totally engaged parent, which probably explained why Steven was such a great kid despite the runaway mother. "If Gerda didn't need you, I'd invite you along."

"That's sweet, but I thought I was supposed to avoid Steven."

Kent stopped halfway out the front door. "I've been thinking about what you said. How it was different with you being his piano teacher." He took her hand, surprising her—but in a good way—as impulses as warm as melted butter on pancakes worked their way up her wrist and arm. "The kid deserves to have fun, and if you're the one who makes him happy, that's all the better. I overreacted. I apologize."

Would surprises ever cease! Maybe she wouldn't have to be on guard every time she was around Steven, and maybe, just maybe, Kent was warming to her company, too?

She didn't want to draw too much attention to his apology and put him on the spot, so she went the flippant route. "Does that mean I can date your son again?" She blinked repeatedly for emphasis, desperately needing to lighten the sexy feelings overtaking her from the mere fact that he held her hand.

He laughed. *Yes, it worked!* "That's taking the cougar thing way too far, isn't it?" He squeezed her hand then let go.

Maybe she'd gone a little too far and should make things completely clear. "So I can give your son a hug without getting dagger eyes from you now, right?"

"I never gave you—"

She imitated the way he'd looked at her, and he got her point.

"Right."

"Thanks." Making progress with Kent and Steven gave her spirits a boost.

"And maybe he isn't the only one you can hug."

With her breath suddenly stolen, she looked into his eyes. That überblue stare nearly undid her as she took in the significance of what he'd said. She could hug Kent, too.

And he hugged her, briefly, but long enough to wake up any lazy nerve endings throughout her body.

Not knowing where to take the conversation next, and thinking it might be best to leave well enough alone, she went for the mundane. "Well, have fun and I hope your team wins."

"Thanks. It'd be even more fun if you could come," he said halfway down the front steps.

That definitely sounded as if he'd had a change of heart. First she was no longer banished from Steven, then she could give both father and son hugs as needed, and now an invitation. "Next time?" *Fingers crossed.*

He kept going. Maybe he was already too far away and hadn't heard her?

Or maybe she'd taken his coming around to her way of thinking beyond his meaning and he conveniently didn't hear her. There was nothing like a dose of reality from being ignored by a proud man walking to his car to put things back into perspective. A man who also happened to be the king of mixed messages.

Kent hung up the phone with Amanda Sunday afternoon. She'd gotten a stomach bug and wouldn't be able to watch Steven. He had the four-to-ten shift tonight, and the last thing he needed was sitter trouble.

He thought about calling Gunnar, in case he was free, but first he needed to go check on Gerda.

It had been hard to see Desi every day, when, if he knew what was good for him, he should put her out of his mind. What was that lame invitation to Steven's basketball game about? He'd been ping-ponging back and forth on Desi ever since he'd met her. His gut told him to go for it, but his brain kept putting on the brakes.

He felt a little like that cartoon character with the devil on one shoulder and an angel on the other. Bottom line, he really needed to figure out what he wanted for Steven and himself first, and then he'd know how to handle adding a woman back into the mix. He was a father now, not a carefree bachelor like Gunnar, who could chase any woman he wanted. Kent was a package deal.

But hadn't Desi said something the other night about having to roll with things sometimes? He couldn't begin to wrap his brain around that concept. It was so not him.

Yet every single time he'd encountered her the past few days, no matter how dressed up or messed up she'd been, she'd taken his breath away. Not good for a man trying to stay on the straight and narrow. A man trying with everything he had to make a normal life for Steven. Family had to come before pleasure.

He tapped on the front door and was surprised and disappointed when Gerda opened it. But considering his mixed-up, messed-up thoughts about Desi, he could use a break.

"Kent! Come in."

"You look great, Gerda." He glanced up when Desi was halfway down the stairs. The July sun had warmed up the temperature, and the sight of her smooth, mocha-colored legs beneath olive-green shorts almost made him drop his stethoscope. "Hey."

"Hey, yourself." She had that playful glint in her eyes that made him wonder if she could read his mind.

He tore away his gaze and escorted Gerda to the couch. "Let's check your blood pressure, okay?"

While he did so, Desi sat on the arm of the couch. Her legs had looked great from across the room, but up close? Man, it took all his willpower to keep his hands to himself.

"You're back to normal," he told Gerda. "Feeling better?"

"Yes. All better. Thank you so much."

His cell phone rang. It was Amanda. "Excuse me. I've got to take this." Unfortunately, she hadn't come through with a substitute babysitter. "Okay, well, thanks for trying. We'll see you Tuesday afternoon."

What was he going to do? He grew serious as he bundled up the blood-pressure machine.

"You look bothered about something," Gerda said.

"I've got sitter problems, and I'm due to work from four to ten tonight."

"I'd be glad to watch Steven for you." Desi spoke right up.

No, he couldn't do that…but exactly why not?

"Now that I'm better, there's no reason Desi can't watch him. Hey, he can have dinner here with us, then she can take him home for his bath and bedtime."

"And I'll make sure he practices his scales. What do you say?"

This wasn't at all what he'd expected to happen when he came over. His smarter self wanted to wait and put a call in to Gunnar before he committed. Truth was, he knew Steven would have a much better time hanging out with Desi and Gerda than at that old bachelor pad of Gunnar's. If he wasn't working, Gunnar probably had a hot date tonight, since his whole world seemed to revolve around his main mistress, his job, and all the other women in town after that.

Kent made a snap decision. "You know what? That would be great. I really appreciate it."

"It's sort of like paying you back for all of these house calls," Desi said, tucking some hair behind her ear, making Kent want to do the same to the other side just for the excuse to touch her.

The payback reasoning was one way to look at it, but he still worried about his son falling too hard for the lovely piano teacher with great legs.

"I'll let him know and send him over when I leave. Thanks."

On his way out the door, thinking about those lovely long legs of Desi's, it occurred to him he should be more concerned about himself, not Steven, falling for her.

Chapter Eight

Kent pulled to the curb just before ten-thirty. In the otherwise dark neighborhood, a few lights were on inside his house, and the anticipation of seeing Desi rushed his pulse. He'd been looking forward to coming home ever since the nine-o'clock lull, when he'd finally had time to think about something other than medicine and sick patients.

He sat an extra few seconds in his car, giving himself a stern talking-to. *Don't make more out of this than it is.* Desi was only doing Steven a favor because she liked him so much. *Whatever you do, don't make a fool of yourself by kissing her again.*

He got out of the car and headed for the front door. Before he could push his key into the lock, it swung open. "Hey," he said, seeing Desi and trying his best to sound nonchalant.

"Hi! I saw you pull up." Desi turned, heading past

the living room toward the kitchen. He'd left the extra house key with Gerda and Desi before he'd left for work.

Desi wore her hair in a high swaying ponytail, and it took only a nanosecond to notice she'd worn his favorite jeans, the ones with little rhinestones in the shape of hearts over each back pocket. A soft-looking loose yellow sweater that slipped off one shoulder—the one she'd worn the first night he'd seen her—rounded out the comfortable but sexy look. She'd kicked off her shoes and those bright red toenails nearly twinkled in the dim light.

She'd made herself at home. Excellent.

Damn, he'd forgotten how great it felt to come home to somebody besides Steven.

"I put Steven to bed at eight-thirty, on the dot." She pointed to her wristwatch with a peach-colored nail.

He put his briefcase on the entry table, reminding himself it wouldn't be appropriate to hug her hello. "Thanks. You saved my life tonight. Don't think my kid would've enjoyed another night in the doctors' lounge watching Sunday-night baseball. And he'd never let me hear the end of it."

"Has that really happened?"

"A couple of times. Sometimes you gotta do what you've gotta do."

"Then I'm especially glad I could help." Desi's eyes sparkled in the hallway light as she walked backward toward the kitchen wearing her signature playful grin. "I baked some cookies. Steven helped. Hope you don't mind."

"They smell great. How many did Steven put away?"

She wrinkled her nose, and now that they were in the bright light of the kitchen, he got close enough to notice those cute tiny freckles across the bridge again. "Half a dozen?"

Kent laughed and shook his head. "And he went to bed without bouncing off the walls?"

She shrugged her shoulders imperceptibly. "Well... he did get up a couple times, but I had him back in bed for good by nine. I hope you don't mind. I've never been in charge of an eight-year-old before."

Kent picked up an oatmeal chocolate chip cookie and took a bite. "Man, these are great. No wonder he ate half a dozen."

Desi turned to the kitchen counter and finished drying the baking items in the dish rack, affording Kent the chance to take in her gorgeous backside again without her noticing. The bling on those pockets, and especially what was beneath, nearly made him drool. He took another cookie and popped it whole into his mouth. The woman could bake, too.

"So how did your night go?" she asked.

How long had it been since he'd been asked that when he'd gotten home? He and Amanda had a total business relationship, very little chitchat. The college student took day classes and needed extra funds, and he desperately needed someone to watch his son after school during the year and summer day camp, five nights a week. That was the extent of their association.

He swallowed the cookie. "Busy but manageable. How about yours?"

"Amusing. He whipped me at Go Fish, and don't even get me started on his computer games. I think he took pity and let me win once. Have I mentioned what a kick I get out of Steven?"

Kent smiled, grateful that his son and the new lady

in town had seemed to click from the start. "He is a great kid."

Evidently Desi liked something about his smile because she stared at him, her eyes lingering on his lips. The cookie was great, but he suddenly wanted to taste *her,* and watching her in his kitchen, acting all domestic, heated up his insides.

Man, oh, man, he couldn't ignore that wide-eyed and welcoming gaze another instant, because those twinkly dark eyes looked as inviting as the semisweet melted chips in the cookies. The question was, what was he going to do about it?

Sure, she was here in Heartlandia only temporarily. Also true, his wife had left him—a crushing blow to his manhood—making him feel more vulnerable where women were concerned than he'd felt in his entire life. The big question was, how did A relate to B?

And what was he going to do about it?

It was hard to think logically with a beautiful, receptive woman such as Desi within reach.

She stood in his kitchen looking superfine with an easygoing expression that practically said, *Well, are you going to kiss me or what?*

What would Gunnar do?

Hands down, he'd go for it.

Kent might be completely out of practice when it came to kissing, but this moment screamed out to be seized, like the other night when he'd kissed her, and he couldn't let this second chance slip away.

Kent put the uneaten portion of his third cookie on the counter and stepped forward. By the lift of her brows, he could tell she suspected what he had in mind. Hell, she'd probably been reading his mind the whole time.

He took Desi by the shoulders, studied her warm and inviting eyes, already getting lost with desire, then planted a quick test kiss smack on her mouth. Probably too abrupt, he chastised himself. What the hell—he wasn't exactly Johnny Depp. Damn, the kiss was great, though, all warm and soft, and the sensations from her lips touching his slowed him down. He inhaled through his nose. In a kitchen filled with fresh-baked cookies, he zeroed in on the fragrance of Polynesian flowers with a hint of apricot that permeated her hair.

She didn't pull away. So far, so good.

He kissed her again.

The first thing to strike him was how soft and full her lips were and how freaking fantastic it was to kiss her. It may have been a little rocky at first, but once they reached their common ground, her soft, persistent kiss nearly melted his belt buckle. As forgotten sensations jetted below his waist, his arms encircled her, and they fit together perfectly. She stretched her fingers around his neck and pulled him closer. Now they were getting somewhere. He deepened the kiss, tasting her sweetness, her tongue testing his.

She was tall and he didn't have to hunch over to kiss her, which was a good thing, and she draped her arms over his shoulders. He also liked that she let him kiss as if he meant it, no matter how rusty he might be. She kissed smooth and natural as breathing, and he followed her guidance, relaxing into the rhythm of making out with her.

Maybe now would be a good time to find and explore those pretty little shiny hearts on each of her cheeks.

He swept his hold downward, skimming over her ribs and waist, admiring the round swells of her plentiful hips, pulling her tight to him. The friction ignited his firewall that carefully guarded his control.

He hadn't wanted a woman like this since long before Diana had left. All the wonder of love and sex seemed to have run its course those last couple of years. Diana had made him feel like a total failure as she withdrew more and more until she'd left. After she'd gone, the subject of making love had been so devastating he couldn't go there. With anyone.

Until now. With Desi.

Heat rolled from his lips in combustible waves all the way down to his toes. He definitely wanted more of this. With her.

"I still owe you that midnight dinner," he said over her mouth.

"I'd like that. Anytime."

Feeling the heat of her body next to his, her warm breath over his chin, his mind went blank for more conversation and he went back to kissing.

Kissing Desi ushered in an overpowering desire to have what a man was meant to share with his woman. Sex. This time, from the way Desi responded to every kiss and touch, it would be with someone new, not Diana, but if he was reading her signals right, it would be with a woman who wanted him as much as he wanted her.

Brakes skidded into gear in his brain, nearly yanking Kent away from another amazing kiss. Did he really want to go there? But he fought off the doubt. Not now. It wasn't as if he was falling in love or anything.

Love meant trusting, and he knew well where trusting a woman led—down a deep hole of pain and regret. But this tornado rolling through his body wasn't love; it was lust, pure and simple, and sex meant only sex. *Right?*

Desi must have sensed his hesitation. She sighed over his lips, snuggled her breasts a little tighter against his chest. His hands gripped her bottom as if hanging on for dear life. *Do not let this moment slip by.*

He hungered for her mouth and body as he dragged his lips along her throat to the quickly beating pulse in her neck. She whimpered a welcoming response.

A guttural sound slipped out of his mouth as his damn brain broke through the firewall again and drew him away from her neck and the shoulder he'd wanted to sample next. He inhaled her scent again then looked into her eyes, seeing concern, but above all confusion.

"Is something wrong?"

He could barely focus on her words for wanting her so much. Need sparked through his body and desire overpowered everything else. He gritted his teeth and inhaled long and hard.

"Is this because of your ex-wife?"

He held on tight, not wanting her to slip from his hold, and silently cussed at the ceiling. No. He shook his head. He'd quit missing his wife half a year ago. But starting up with someone new rattled the hell out of him.

Grow a pair, Larson!

"You'll be leaving at some point, too," he said, choosing the *honesty is the best policy* route.

Desi went up on her tiptoes to capture his lips for a few more seconds of bliss. She pulled back and played with the collar of his shirt. Her thick-lashed lids fluttered up and down. "That may be true, but I'm not running away tonight."

He'd never had a fling. He was the guy who went steady all his life and married the girl right out of college. This was completely out of his realm of understanding, except his body was sending an entirely different message than his overactive and protective brain.

WWGD? What would Gunnar do? Go for it, idiot! You're allowed to have sex with a beautiful and willing partner.

Kent pulled her back to his chest, his mouth seeking the fine skin of her cheeks and ears, inhaling the fresh tropical-and-apricot scent in her hair again. His wandering hands couldn't feel her everywhere fast enough. He pressed his erection against her waist, sending a shock of lust all the way to his spine. She moaned and moved closer against him.

When he looked into her eyes, he saw all the want, heat and need he felt mirrored there, and the decision was made. "Let's go. That is, if you want—"

"Definitely." Desi smiled, taking his hand, and, now that he'd gotten her consent, they practically jogged toward his bedroom. Before they hit the stairs, she tugged back, stopping him. "What's wrong with the couch?"

Maybe she worried about Steven's bedroom being so close upstairs? She couldn't possibly know the boy was a notoriously sound sleeper.

"Great." Giving thanks for the Victorian-style house with the French doors closing off the living room, he instantly changed course. Why waste another moment away from her body?

Her sweater slipped easily over her shoulders and through the matching yellow bra he could make out her nipples. He swallowed in deep appreciation, parched from wanting her so damn much. He couldn't yank off his shirt fast enough. There was longing in her eyes when she stared at his bare chest, her tongue wetting her bottom lip.

Within seconds they'd peeled off the rest of their clothes and hit the cushions in a heated skin-to-skin tangle. Her soft curves and his tight angles came together in a rush of desire so strong they practically bumped heads and knees, but nothing would stop them from their mission. She'd landed on top and he caressed and sampled her lush breasts, savoring their weight and feel, teasing the velvety dark tips with his tongue until they peaked even tighter.

She was beyond beautiful, the kitchen light silhouetting her body like solar flares. A tropical-scented goddess. Her hands were as eager as his and they explored his chest and stomach, and the building sensations beneath her fingers begged for more of her touches. More. And more.

His erection stood tall, fully engorged, pulsing at her center. She straddled his waist and he found her entrance with his fingers, coaxing her open, amazed at how ready she felt for him. His hands were on each side of her hips, on the verge of lifting her high enough to take him inside, when his brain called out for sanity.

"Condom. Damn it." Did he even have them anymore?

Desi wrapped her hand around him and squeezed gently. Sparklers went off behind his lids. "Hurry back."

He'd find one of those suckers if he had to dig through a trash can.

He moved her aside and stood. "Do. Not. Move." With one last wet kiss, he left her grinning behind closed doors. She was naked on the couch, her hair wild, making her look like an astral queen. He could imagine the senior Life Art class busting at the seams with students when word got out she'd posed for them, and he laughed inwardly as he threw on his slacks and headed for the second floor.

His good fortune at meeting her, having her waiting for him, propelled him up the stairs to his medicine cabinet. Nada. Damn it all to hell. Just his luck to have the most exotically beautiful woman he'd ever seen waiting and…

Hold on! His briefcase. He always kept samples of medicine from the drug companies on hand to give to patients who couldn't afford to pay for prescriptions. He also kept a batch of condoms to give out for the same reason. Tiptoeing past Steven's room just in case the cookies messed with his usual sleeping pattern, he rushed back down the stairs. He made a beeline for his briefcase and, thanking the aligning stars in heaven, found a few stragglers. He chose a neon yellow one, thinking about her discarded sweater and bra. The wrapper said "extra lubrication." From the way she'd felt, it wasn't necessary, but on second thought he grabbed a handful.

Practically growling from desire zinging through him, he found her right where he'd left her. Dropping his pants and quickly stepping out, he held her face in his palms and kissed her soundly. She tasted silky and sweet, delicious like those cookies. Her body melded to his, warming him through and through. Hot humming pulsated inside every cell in his body as he kissed his way down to her waist. He inhaled her woman scent and kissed her between her soft folds, enjoying her special taste as she writhed beneath his touch. Her throaty response made him wild with the need to satisfy her. He glanced up. She muffled the escalating moans by biting her lip and turning her head into the couch cushion until she came, her fingers digging into his scalp as she did.

Good thing a cruise ship could blast the horn for an hour yet never disturb the super-sound-sleeper Steven.

Kent couldn't stand another second without being buried inside her, and from the way she pawed at him, pulling and dragging him over her, she needed him, too. Her hands guided him to her entrance, then straight on to heaven on earth. She was tight and warm and slick and…

He couldn't think anymore. Every pent-up feeling he'd stockpiled over the past year fought to break free. All that existed was the feel of her, the dive and roll of their bodies and the building feral sensations. Single-minded in his quest, he thrust and pulled back, again and again, faster and faster, sensations building toward atomic fusion. Time disappeared. It was just them. Their bodies.

Crying out, she spasmed around him as the rhythmic, tightening aftershocks launched him on toward bliss. And he was gone.

But he kept thrusting with a guttural groan, their bodies tight, nuclear hot and wet against each other, and she came again, sweetening the final throes of the most amazing orgasm he'd ever had.

Desi couldn't believe what had just happened. The man who never wanted her near his son had just gifted her with a triple-header! Her body, still wide-awake to Kent's every touch, still pulsing with leftover sensations, had never felt more alive. She dug her fingers into her hair and stretched like a cat, savoring the feel. He sat and smiled down at her.

Even from this angle he was gorgeous. His wide smile stretched nearly from ear to ear, and those smoldering *I just did you good* eyes stoked a new round of tingles. He was a complete package of near perfection with broad shoulders, developed pecs dusted in light hair, muscular arms and abs that belonged on a magazine cover. How had she gotten so lucky?

"You okay?" he asked.

She inhaled through her nose, taking her time to respond. "I've never been better. You?"

He sputtered a laugh. "Damn, woman, you're hot." He cupped her hip and patted.

She went up on her elbows so she could reach his lips and gave him a peck. "Thank you."

They kissed as if they hadn't seen each other in months, eager to lock lips again and get lost in each other. His hands worked wonders on her skin, conjuring gooseflesh everywhere he touched. Her tightening nipples sent fleeting messages to her core, still simmering from sex. *Be on the ready.*

She could get lost in Kent, again and again.

He stretched out beside her, wrapping one arm around her waist, his thighs flush to her side. She sampled his glorious firm glutes. The man truly had to be a descendant of Vikings.

"Can I get you some water?" He stood, the last of his erection in evidence.

"Love it. I'm dying of thirst."

He smiled at her with those heavy-lidded eyes, rekindling her desire as if they'd never been together tonight. She glanced at her watch, the only thing she still wore. How long could she stay here before Grandma might get suspicious?

Still flying from their lovemaking, she was nowhere near ready to figure out what any of this meant. She watched with total fascination as he walked to the kitchen, handsomeness in motion.

While he was gone, she lay there, with one thought on her mind: Where did they go from here?

A quick minute later, when he'd obviously gone to the bathroom and cleaned up, he returned with one tall glass of water. She took it and sipped. When she offered him some, he took a drink. Their gazes met and held. There went that nuclear-fusion thing again smack-dab in the middle of her belly, and soon the water was on the coffee table and completely forgotten. Their only thirst was for each other, and they reacquainted themselves with each other's bodies, one touch at a time.

Chapter Nine

Midmorning Monday, Desi went into town specifi-
cally to talk to Cliff Lincoln. She'd bonded with him in
more ways than the color of their skin and wanted his
advice. She knew he'd be in the kitchen whipping up his
luncheon special, so she went around to the back. The
door was open and the wondrous aroma of simmering
onions, garlic and green peppers made her mouth water.

"Knock, knock," she said, eyeing Cliff at the extra-
large gas stove, stirring the contents in a thick iron pot.

He turned and broke into a toothy grin. "Well, well,
if it isn't Desdemona Rask."

"Is it okay if I come in?"

"Sure. Put your feet up, take a load off those dogs.
I'll pour us some coffee."

Cliff made Desi feel as at home in his restaurant
kitchen as Gerda did at home. Combined with her hot
next-door neighbor, Heartlandia was beginning to have

a hold on her. The good kind. *Would it make you happy, Mom, to know I've found some peace of mind in the place you ran away from?* Somehow it didn't seem right. Could these feelings turn into a stranglehold like they had for her mother? The mixed-up thoughts confused her.

"I wanted to thank you for sending over that delicious soup the other night."

"Ms. Gerda Rask, besides being our mayor, is a fine woman of the community. She'd do the same for me and mine." He handed Desi a thick mug full to the brim, remembering and including the creamer. "That's Louisiana's finest right there."

Desi smiled, nodding her head in thanks, taking the cup with both hands and inhaling the potent coffee.

"What brings you around today?"

She scrunched up her nose, not knowing how to begin. "I've just been wondering…" She blew into her mug and took a quick sip of the strong, bitter brew. "How did you know Heartlandia was the place for you?"

Cliff stopped stirring, a wise expression consuming his face. "Ah, the sixty-four-thousand-dollar question." He nailed her with a one-eyed squint. "You thinking of moving in with your grandmother for good?"

She shrugged. "First I've got to find my father."

"Is that so?"

"I think it's important that I do. But maybe I'll come back."

"Right. Right." He turned off the gas flame and moved the pot to the side, then leaned against the counter and folded his arms. "So you want to know how I knew Heartlandia was the place for me. Here's the long answer. As soon as I turned eighteen I joined the navy, went around the world, then got hired on the cruise line. I guess you could say I'd been a vagabond my whole life." He picked up his mug and drank heartily. "There was just something special about Heartlandia right from the start. Every time that cruise ship docked and I came ashore, the people here didn't look at me like I planned to mug them like in so many other cities around the world. They didn't seem to care that I was black. I liked the Scandinavian feel, the beautiful trees, the gracious people and the river. It felt like home. I never get tired of looking at the Columbia River. It brought me here, and if I ever want to leave, it will take me away."

It felt like home. What does home feel like?

"You met your wife here, too, right?"

"Oh, yes, but not right away. She's twenty years younger." He gave the smile of a proud man who'd snagged a younger woman. "I worked this restaurant hard for five years, barely keeping afloat. Then I hired this sweet young thing right out of high school as a waitress, and she suggested I cook some soul food. Worked like a charm, got more cruise customers and word spread. *Try the gumbo at Lincoln's Place in Heartlandia. Check out his shrimp and grits.* She had a good head on her shoulders and she fell in love with me to prove it." He pursed his lips, trying to look humble but failing miserably. "Course, it took me a while to notice. Anyway, by then Heartlandia was my home, and I haven't wanted to leave, not once."

Desi envied his conviction. Sure she liked it here. Loved Gerda. Didn't know where she stood with Kent, but, man, she wasn't anywhere near ready to walk away from that sexy gift. But did it feel like home?

She'd made herself a promise to find her father, to learn about her roots. To figure out who she truly was.

"You want some pie or somethin'?"

"Nah, I'm good." Desi drank more of the coffee. "I've got some errands to run for Gerda since she has meetings all day, and I need some calligraphy supplies."

"You think any more about playin' the piano on weekends for me?"

Truth was, she had been thinking about it a lot. She'd even been practicing all of her favorite Scott Joplin rags and more Ellington, too, but wasn't ready to admit it to Cliff or commit to staying. She really needed to find her father, see where that led first. "Maybe a little."

"A little playin' or a little *thinkin'* 'bout playin'? Which one?"

"I've been thinking about whether or not I want to work for you."

"But you need to find your father first, right?"

She gave a wry smile and took another sip of coffee.

"What you expect to 'discover'?" He used air quotes. "That you're an African princess? That you've got a dozen brothers and sisters all waiting their whole lives just to meet you? To get in touch with your soulful side?"

He'd rubbed her the wrong way. "You don't have to put it that way."

"Maybe I do. Maybe I need you to understand that you're already Desdemona Rask. You already know who you are, whether you realize it or not."

She didn't look at him. Couldn't he understand there was more to it than that? She'd never met her father. She needed to learn about the rest of her heritage.

"I don't want to burst your bubble, but odds are you'd

be an intrusion into someone's complicated life. If there's a wife involved, it might really tick her off. Maybe you should be ready for that possibility."

"That may be true, but I still need to find out, Cliff."

"Yes, you do, little sister. If you say so, but I'm trying to tell you, it won't change who you already are. Don't become one of those people who're always looking for something else and forget to notice what's right in front of them. Take it from me—it's a waste of time."

Cliff gave her a dose of reality that didn't go down nearly as well as the strong coffee, but she couldn't give up until she found the man who'd changed Ester Rask's life forever. Maybe he'd change her life, too.

She stood, finished off her coffee and put the mug in the huge stainless-steel sink. "I hear what you're saying, but…"

"—but you've just got to find out. I know. I know. And I wish you well. You know I do." He turned the burner on again and went back to sautéing the vegetables. "If you decide to work for me, just let me know."

Cliff had played the devil's advocate, the voice of reason, and she needed to think about all the possible scenarios she could face when meeting her father. In his own gruff way, Cliff showed he cared. Heck, he'd offered her a job right from the start.

The notion came over her out of nowhere, but without giving it further thought, she crossed the kitchen and hugged him from behind.

"Thank you."

Surprise made his nearly black eyes open wide and his lips stretch into a large smile as he turned around and hugged her back with the non-sautéing arm. "Anytime, li'l bit. Anytime." He squeezed her close to his soft middle then set her free.

Desi left him smiling and humming to himself, a contented man who knew exactly who he was no matter where he lived. Even if he was the only black man in town. She, on the other hand, felt more restless and out of touch with herself than when she'd walked in.

She cornered the alley to his restaurant and got back on the main street. It was a beautiful sunny day and downtown Heartlandia looked like something off a book cover—clean, colorful and self-contained.

Thinking about clean and colorful, she was reminded of the interior of Kent's house, and how it definitely had a woman's touch when it came to decorating. If that was the case, his ex-wife had impeccable taste with a perfect mix of French country and small-town charm. The sage-green living room had complementary print wingback chairs on either side of a tall, modern rock fireplace. The deep red microfiber wraparound couch with the chaise-lounge end was perfect for their lovemaking last night. All the hardwood floors were in mint condition and extended into the buttery-yellow kitchen with brown granite counters and copper pots and pans hanging over the island. It looked right out of a magazine. The bland white exterior of the house gave the wrong impression. Kent's house was warm and homey, and she'd gotten too comfortable there too quickly.

Deep in thought, she almost didn't notice the police car drive by and slow to a stop. Out popped Kent's friend Gunnar. "How's it going?"

"Oh, hi. Good. How about you?"

"Doing well." The way he smiled at her made her wonder if he knew about her and Kent already. Did men kiss and tell like ladies did? If she had a best friend, she'd have spilled all the details about something that amazing in record time. "I guess I'm not much of a pinch-hitting friend for Kent, so thanks for stepping up with babysitting yesterday."

"Of course. That's what neighbors are for." Warmth invaded her cheeks. Did he know just how much she'd "stepped up" already?

"Uh, hey, the police station is just down the street if you ever feel like stopping by. I'll show you around."

Or was the guy hitting on her? "Thanks." She fidgeted with the strap of her shoulder bag. "Well, I don't want to hold you up or anything."

He may have tried to be subtle, but he looked her over good before getting back into the car. Just before he did, he tipped his hat with a suave smile.

Seeing Gunnar put Kent front and center in her thoughts again as she walked down the street toward The Paper Mill. She'd thought about their lovemaking all night. He'd satisfied every single cell in her body, and she'd gone home feeling like Jell-O. Her pulse went a little wacky remembering everything they'd done.

On a nonsexual note, she'd been grossly unfair to him considering his circumstances. She'd expected him to be completely well-adjusted, even after finding out his wife had left, making him a reluctant single father. She'd been impatient and put out by his overprotective ways with Steven, but wouldn't she have done the same thing in his shoes?

The last thing she could claim was being well-adjusted. Was she chasing a dream searching for her father, as Cliff had said? Her roots? If she really wanted to find him, how come she hadn't even tried to look him up yet? Hmm, maybe Gunnar could help out in that department.

Desi stepped inside The Paper Mill, heading right to the pens and special-paper section.

"Hi, Desi!" the clerk said.

What was with this town? She'd been in the store only one other time, introduced herself as the mayor's granddaughter, and the little bird-framed, blue-haired lady in a homemade knitted sweater behind the counter already remembered her. She waved and smiled.

After purchasing her items, she left hugging her bag, heading for the market with Gerda's list, wondering if it was a good or a bad thing to live in such a small town.

Monday evening, Kent tapped on the Rask screen door. Steven stood by his side, antsy. Kent copped to being nervous about seeing the woman he'd thought about all day at work, but couldn't stay away.

It was warmer today, and the inside door was open, affording him his first glimpse of Desi as a silhouette sauntering from the kitchen. Need sparked through him when she opened the screen and smiled. How many times had he thought about the way she laughed, light and breezy, how great she'd felt, how tenderly she'd kissed him? How she'd satisfied him beyond his wildest dreams.

She wore those crazy big hoop earrings today, and the lush glow of peach gloss on her smooth lips. He wanted to kiss her right there in front of Steven but fought the impulse. There was an extra charge in her gaze as she looked at him, and he hoped it was because she might want to kiss him, too.

"You wanna go have dinner with us?" Steven jumped the gun.

She tore away from their staring match, eyes darting to Steven. "Oh, I'd love to, but Gerda is feeling so much better she's teaching me how to make fish balls. You want to eat here?"

Steven screwed up his tiny nose. "No, thanks. Dad promised me a burger and milk shake."

"Aw, shoot. I wish I could go, but you know…"

"I know. Mayor Rask is old and she needs company."

Kent suppressed his laugh. "Now, Steven." The boy could blurt the most outrageous things. The twinkle in Desi's eyes proved she enjoyed his innocent faux pas, too. Her thoughtful gaze wandered up to Kent's.

He didn't want to appear too eager in front of his son. "If it's okay, I'll stop by later."

"I'd like that."

"I'm all ready for my piano lesson," Steven chimed in, oblivious to the full-out attraction arcing in the air between his father and the new piano teacher. "You're going to be proud of me."

"I'm sure I am," she said.

"So you better have an extra-special treat."

She laughed and Kent thought he'd never get enough of her generous and friendly ways where his son was concerned. Or her natural beauty, her golden-bronze skin, round curves and wide fawnlike eyes.

"Okay, we're out of here," Kent said, before his body could get out of hand.

Desi waved goodbye, and he checked his watch to see how long before he could have some time alone with her again. Every minute would seem like an hour. No doubt about it, Steven was going to bed at eight tonight, no excuses. "You can't tell your piano teacher how to reward you," he said, walking down the path to his truck.

"Why not?"

"That's not the way it works." Though the concept wasn't half-bad. Kent let a quick fantasy flicker through his brain of the many ways he'd like to tell Desi how to reward *him*.

At eight-fifteen he strode out the door, heading for the Rask place. Desi must have read his mind because she was sitting on the porch reading. The thought of having a few moments alone with her made his pulse race. A few months ago, he'd never expected anything like this could ever happen again.

She offered that picture-perfect smile of hers the whole while he walked up the porch stairs and across the distance to where she sat.

"Hey," he said.

"Hi."

He wanted her to stand up so he could hug her, make contact as soon as possible. Again, as if she read his mind, she stood. He welcomed her into his arms and let the wonder of holding a woman close again register in his body.

"You look pretty," he said, kissing her hair, remembering how that tropical scent had stuck in his mind all day at work.

"Thank you." Her hands rubbed his back, rushing his pulse even more. She looked up, those lush lips there for the taking. Wanting to devour her, he practiced self-control and dropped a quick hello kiss on her mouth instead.

Don't make her uncomfortable. Just because you

*want to jump her bones doesn't mean she feels the same.
She's a whole person, someone you want to do things
for, someone you want to know better.*

He let her go and sat on the love seat. She snuggled
close, and her warmth kept his pulse thumping fast and
hard.

"I ran into Gunnar today in town," she said.

"You did?"

"Yeah. He seems nice. Made me wonder if there
might be some way he could help me locate my father."
Her honesty about needing to find her birth father made
his stomach knot. He'd let his guard down and had sex
with her. So it was just sex for her, too, a little gift to
help him get beyond the incredibly lousy year he'd survived, nothing more. He shouldn't be feeling this way,
a little lost, empty and worried. Damn, he didn't know
how to do casual.

"I don't have a clue how to start looking for him."

"Well, maybe Gunnar can point you in the right direction." It hurt to say it, especially since that direction might lead her out of town, away from him, but he
wanted to help her.

"That's what I was thinking."

"You sure you don't want to stick around Heartlandia
and live with Gerda?"

"I'm not sure of anything, but I made myself a promise to find that man. See where it leads."

It could lead her right out of town to never come
back, and the idea gripped his gut, making it feel as if
his belt buckle had tightened a notch. That was how it
had started with his wife, too, one little step at a time
until she was gone for good. Feeling already in over
his head, he found it hard to breathe. Maybe it was a

big mistake to have sex with her. Why the hell couldn't he do casual?

"Dad?" Steven's voice carried across the narrow yard from his front door.

"I'm right here."

"I had a bad dream."

"Coming." As he got up, Desi joined him. He gave her a quick kiss goodbye in the shadows so Steven couldn't see. The treat he'd been looking forward to all day had grown complicated and now got cut short. His need to control the situation fought with the way things were playing out. All he wanted was some more time with Desi, and all she wanted was to take off looking for her father. "Good night."

She didn't say it back, and he could see that sassy glint in her eyes. Maybe things were looking up. She shot up on her tippy-toes and kissed him a beat or two longer. A kiss that promised more than good-night. "I'll see you later," she whispered.

Kent's mood lifted, and he took the stairs then strode across the yard toward his house, grinning, a sexy buzz vibrating through his body. On this count he definitely liked the way Desi Rask thought.

Around ten, light tapping came from the front door. Waiting for Desi, he'd been reading a medical journal on the latest superbacteria and had lost track of time.

He opened the door. Desi stood on his doorstep bright-eyed and as refreshing as the evening breeze, and she nearly took his breath away. She rushed into his arms. Their earlier conversation about her still wanting to find her dad may have been a cold shower to his brain, but not his body. He kissed her the way he'd wanted to earlier, and her mouth welcomed him. With their bodies wrapped tight, they made out for several more minutes. He loved lifting her hair and kissing the spots on her neck and shoulders that made her purr. He couldn't get enough of that Polynesian-flower scent in her hair. It had messed with his mind all day at work.

Her hands couldn't seem to get enough of him, either, and his body went directly into conquer mode.

As things heated up, his thoughts got out of hand. Before he could censor himself, he broke from their kiss. "I just want to say one thing."

Her first answer was another mind-jumbling kiss. "Lay it on me."

"I want you to consider staying in Heartlandia."

Desi had never felt more wanted in her life. A huge and gorgeous hunk of man was hot for her and asking her to stick around. When had that ever happened before? Never. She'd promised her mother she'd go to her grandmother's, but she'd promised herself to go even further—to find her dad. She didn't have a clue if he was even still alive, but now was the time to make the journey.

Kent kissed her again, and her thoughts turned to mush. Men knew how to disconnect emotions from sex. If they could, so could she. It was probably for the best.

But Kent's comment gave the impression he wasn't any better at it than she was. *I want you to consider staying in Heartlandia.*

"Maybe you should shut up and kiss me," she said, avoiding his question and going right for his mouth. Kent didn't need coaxing. Nope, she was completely aware of his firm response and it was pressing into her belly. She'd made an extra stop in town today, at the drugstore, and came prepared with a couple of condoms of her own. She wondered when Kent's hand roamed to her bottom if he'd notice the wrappers tucked inside her jeans pocket.

"Did I mention my kid sleeps like a rock?"

With fire in those natural bedroom eyes, he took her hand and led her upstairs, straight to his king-size bed, where he slowly undressed her and laid her down, soon joining her after shedding his clothes.

It's just sex, she told herself, but Kent had a look on his face that communicated something more. His hands were slow and thoughtful as they explored, his every touch intentional. She quivered as he caressed her, as he worshipped her breasts and belly and the sweet spot between her legs.

She could get used to this.

Just sex, Desi, just casual sex.

They came together and she got the distinct impression he was offering so much more than sex this time. Or she'd distorted this perfect little setup of hooking up with the sexy doc next door, had read into it, made it out to be more than what it was. S. E. X.

He kissed her then looked deep into her eyes as he stroked in and out. The intimacy threw her. Staring into his baby blues, she knew it wasn't just sex. He'd asked her to think about sticking around, and he was making her dizzy with that intensely sexy gaze.

She closed her eyes and shut down her brain, letting their bodies do all the communicating. And as the moments clicked by, he knew exactly how to take her all the way.

At midnight, sated from making love with Kent, she gathered her clothes to head for home. The last thing she wanted was for either Steven or Gerda to find out what she and Kent had been up to.

He lay on his stomach with the sheet over his waist, his tousled blond hair sexy as hell, his jaw relaxed and eyes closed, his broad back dappled by moonlight. A gorgeous sight.

An ache planted itself behind her chest, and it had nothing to do with the stupendous sex they'd shared. Longing for something she'd never had before—a real relationship—left a bittersweet taste in her mouth. Was she one foot in or out of Heartlandia?

Their timing was off. But maybe down the road after she'd found her father and discovered the other half of herself, after she finally knew who she was, and Kent had enough time to completely move on from his divorce, maybe then they could make whatever this was work.

Wanting nothing more than to climb right back into bed and cuddle up with Kent, Desi got dressed, tiptoed out of the room and padded across the yard to her grandmother's house.

Once in bed, she savored the way it felt to be wanted for the first time in her adult life, and to help soothe her brain for sleep, she pretended things didn't have to be different.

Chapter Ten

"My arthritis seems to have settled down," Gerda said. "I think I'm ready to take over the piano students again."

Gerda and Desi shared the piano bench Tuesday morning, having just practiced a duet together for fun. Gerda had suggested it after tending to a few morning mayoral duties. Sunlight streamed through the side windows, making everything look golden. Desi wanted to imprint the moment in her mind as a special memory.

"Are you sure, Grandma?"

"I've missed them. Those students added purpose to my life long before I became mayor. Besides, I've been thinking too much about our pirate problems." She'd hushed her voice when she'd said "pirate problems," as though the walls had ears. "I need to get my mind on something else."

"How's that going?" Desi studied the thin skin of

Gerda's hands as they rested on the piano keys, the pencil-point-thin blue veins beneath.

Her hands flew to her lap and knotted. "Elke Norling is deciphering the journals, and she'll report back at the next meeting."

"Deciphering? Isn't it in English?

"Have you ever seen Old English? It's like another language. *S* looks like *F,* and there's all kinds of extra swirliques—I don't know what to call them, but you know what I mean. His cursive is poor at best, and much of the ink has smeared or faded."

"I get it. It's nothing like we write today."

"Yes, and it's one big whopping job for someone who has a full-time position at the city college." Lines fanned from the corners of Gerda's eyes as she smiled at Desi. "Some of us still hold out hope that Captain Nathaniel Prince—" she put her hand over her mouth and spoke to the side toward Desi "—also known as the Prince of Doom, did his terrible deeds somewhere else and maybe only shipwrecked around here. Everything has to be verified. We'll see what Elke reports at the next meeting."

"Captain Nathaniel Prince. Hmm." Desi made a quick sketch of how the Prince of Doom might have looked. Not being very imaginative this morning, she figured he looked a lot like Jack Sparrow.

Gerda shook her head and sighed. "Yes, he was captain of a treacherous ship called *Neptune's Fortune,* according to the initial information we've gleaned from that chest. For all we know, it could be sunken somewhere near Heartlandia." Her hand went to her breast. "God, I hope not."

"But wouldn't it be cool if that sunken ship had buried treasure? Think of the tourists who would flock to see it."

"That's a major concern. We don't want to upset our community. We love things just the way they are. And if and when we make our decision about what to do, it will all land on my shoulders as mayor pro tem to deliver the news to the Heartlandians."

Though Desi was entirely amused by the possibility of her newfound hometown possibly being tainted by wicked pirates, she also understood the grave disappointment her grandmother felt about the historical black eye to her beloved Heartlandia. Besides, Desi had rocked her grandmother's world enough lately simply by showing up. Maybe it was time to change the subject, before Gerda started grabbing her chest again and needing sedatives.

"I was wondering," Desi said as she slipped her arm around her grandmother and drew her close. "Would it be okay if I kept on with Steven?"

"Of course. You've brought him so far along in just a few weeks. It's nothing short of amazing."

"And he is your last student today, which will give me plenty of time to prepare before his lesson."

"Are you going somewhere?"

"It's Kent's day off, and he offered to take me on a tour of the city college and the Ringmiren wall, so it really is convenient for you to take over the first lessons today."

Gerda clapped. "Oh, how wonderful. I should have taken you there myself, but…"

"You've been really busy, Grandma. Not to mention not feeling well."

"True." Gerda looked into Desi's eyes, hope shining in her own. "Are you and Kent dating?"

Could Desi call it "dating," or maybe she should say they were neighbors with benefits? She felt a blush coming on. "I'm not sure what we're doing, but he's a super-nice guy." *And, oh, he's so much more than that. He's an outrageous lover and a fabulous father, a respected doctor and...* "And he needs a break from his routine as much as anyone, don't you think? So when he suggested showing me around, I jumped at it."

"Well, I, for one, couldn't be happier."

That was what had been nagging Desi, too. She hadn't been this happy in...well, a long, long time, and she knew it wouldn't continue, not if she went searching for her father. Which she still really and truly needed to do.

After a late lunch outside at the Fika Bakery, Desi relaxed back in her chair, enjoying the sunshine and Kent's handsome face. The awning cast sharp shadows over his profile. She watched the grooves that formed on either side of his nose and mouth when he smiled, straight teeth peeking out from between his lips. The lips she'd made out with under a pine tree and leaning against the Ringmiren wall only a half hour ago.

Watching him made her heart tighten. It wasn't the usual feeling she had when dating a guy, that was for sure.

He'd started growing a beard along his jawline, which was brown in contrast to his blond hair. The finely manicured beard, mustache and soul patch curtained the edge of his jaw and lips, making him look chiseled and gorgeous. She liked how the new mustache tickled when they kissed. Combined with that dashing smile and those heavy-lidded blue eyes shining her way, one word surfaced in her brain. *Sexy.* Then two words—*scary sexy.* As she took in the full picture of the man—with a gentle smile only for her—a warm ball of want curled deep inside her.

He took her hand and squeezed. Was he thinking what she was thinking? The first signs of desire coiled tighter.

"I've got an idea," he said.

Oh, yes, they were on the same page.

"I'm up for anything." Desi went for coy and a double entendre.

"How about I take you—"

Take me, yes—exactly what I was thinking.

"—to the police station. Maybe Gunnar can help you out with your dad."

Not what I had in mind, but, what? You want to help me find my dad?

"Wow. That would be great." How could she refuse his generous offer?

The police station was larger than she expected and it was in the same building as the local newspaper. The standard concrete facade was decorated with huge columns on either side of the entrance. Marble floors in the foyer echoed as they turned left and headed for the bank of floor-to-ceiling windows under the Heartlandia Police Department banner and official emblem. She wondered, since it was a police station, if the glass was bulletproof.

It was stuffy inside, and Desi was nervous, but Kent held her hand and guided her to the desk.

"Is Sergeant Norling here?"

At the sound of his name, and before the young, narrow-necked desk clerk could answer, Gunnar's head popped around a corner. His face brightened at the sight of Kent. "Hey, I thought I recognized your voice. Come on back." He pushed something under the counter that released the lock and Kent was able to open the door at the end of the desk. They shook hands and patted each other's backs affectionately.

"You remember Desi, right?"

Gunnar nodded at Desi with a fleeting knowing glance. "Sure do. How you been?" he asked, even though they'd just seen each other yesterday. He shook her hand. His grip was firm and rough around the edges, nothing like Kent's.

"I'm good. Thanks." She let go a beat before he did, edging closer to Kent and away from the imposing figure in the *don't mess with me* uniform. Which, she noted, fit him to a tee and outlined a striking figure. Muscular guys, however, were not her type. At all.

"Hey," Kent broke in. "Desi is trying to locate her father. All she has is a name, a ballpark birth date and a last-known address."

"He was a jazz musician," she said. "Played with some biggies. Don't know if that will help at all."

"I can't use our database for something like that." Gunnar scratched his cheek, noticing Desi's obvious disappointment. "But I know a guy in Portland who's a P.I., and he specializes in this exact thing. Finding people." He strode to his desk and flipped through his Rolodex. "Yeah, here's the guy."

Desi caught his eager-to-please expression and smiled. "Do you think he'd help me? How much does he cost?"

After a surreptitious glance toward Kent, Gunnar

lifted a brow, engaging Desi again. "He owes me a favor. Tell you what—give me the information and I'll have him run a check on your father. If he finds anything, I'll get back to you."

"That'd be great," Kent said, touching Desi's heart by his generosity of spirit, arranging this meeting and helping in the search for her birth father. That unusual feeling she sometimes got when she looked at Kent swelled once again in her chest.

Desi wrote down everything she knew about her father, which struck her as so meager and sad, and handed it to Gunnar along with her cell-phone number.

Kent had made it very clear as they toured the city college that he thought Desi should stick around Heartlandia, try out some classes at the school, give them a chance to get to know each other better. The idea struck her as especially appealing.

Did he want more than great sex? Might he feel that same strange sensation about her that she always got when she thought about him? *Don't get carried away.*

Kent looked at his watch. "Oh, hey, it's almost time to pick up Steven from summer day camp. We've got to run."

After a quick goodbye, Desi followed Kent out of the station house, and taking his hand, she rushed along with his brisk pace back to the car.

How normal it felt to be with the man she had definite feelings for, rushing off to get his son. A quick snapshot of the future, a hope and dream she'd never realized she'd had before, popped into her head.

"So I guess we'll just wait and see what happens about your father," he said, shoving the key in the ignition, making a point not to look at her.

Firmly back in reality, she switched out of fantasy gears.

Maybe helping her locate her father wasn't selfless generosity after all. Maybe it was his way of trying to take control of the situation. Or maybe it was a test.

Later that night, after Gerda had gone to bed, Desi stole across the yard to Kent's, unable to stay away. It was after ten, they'd been texting, and he was waiting for her. He opened the door wearing a broad grin, shirtless on the warm night. They came together in a hot embrace and that growing desire she'd put on hold earlier in the day came back to life.

She'd decided to keep her involvement with Kent a secret from her grandmother, to let her think they were merely dating, not sleeping with each other. Desi didn't want to disappoint Gerda or change her old-style attitude toward Kent. Oh, but making love with Kent Larson seemed like so much more than secret sex. Especially now, with his mouth warm on her lips and his hands slipping up and down her sides, igniting every cell along her skin.

A little after midnight, Desi lay naked and cuddled under Kent's arm, her head resting on his chest. Each of his contented breaths lifted her head ever so gently. He played with her hair, tickling her neck with it.

"You know, you really should give some thought to enrolling in a few classes this fall." Knowing she'd protest like she had when they were on campus earlier, he covered her mouth with his free hand. She playfully bit a finger.

"You should quit telling me what to do."

"And I think playing piano for Cliff's restaurant is a great idea. You're a gifted pianist—why not share it for others to enjoy?"

She knocked her knuckles lightly on his temple, wishing she hadn't shared Cliff's job offer with Kent. "Did you hear what I just said?"

"Then you could work part-time while you're taking classes."

She let her feigned protest rest. His complete trust in her capabilities and confidence in her talent made her want to please him, want to show him she could do anything she set out to do, just like her mother had always said. She admitted his having a plan all mapped out for her was sweet to a certain extent. But it was her life, and she had every intention of making her own decisions about it.

Not having a father, and her dating life up to now being far from ideal, she'd never had a man believe in her before. The way Kent's hands roamed aimlessly across her shoulders, drawing her close for a tender hug, she believed him. Maybe he cared about her as more than a sexual partner. Maybe he wanted her in his life beyond the bedroom.

Maybe she should take a chance, stick around, let herself fall for him and settle down for good in Heartlandia. She kissed his chest, splayed her fingers across his defined pecs, wishing she could trust her growing desire to stay here.

Maybe it was too good to be true.

The hungry demons inside gnawed at her self-esteem. They insisted she was two halves of a whole and couldn't be a complete person until she found the other half. She was biracial to Kent's pure Scandinavian. She wasn't educated compared to him. She wasn't refined, didn't have a clue what she wanted to do with her life. If they took this bedroom affair into daylight, where he could get a really good look at her, she'd probably disappoint him.

Then what would she do? She couldn't very well live next door to a man who didn't accept her. A man who'd break her heart.

"Where are you?" Kent's gentle voice pulled her away from the negativity bombs crashing around her, and his arms tugged her farther up his chest.

She sighed, trying to empty her head.

He lifted her chin and brushed his lips across hers. Their eyes met. And held. The smoldering look undid her.

"Stay with me," he said, deepening the kiss. "Just a while longer."

That familiar and indescribable warm feeling coursed through her veins when she knew without a doubt he wanted her. Like now. She let all the questions and doubts about her future evaporate as their bodies interlaced perfectly, as they always did. And finally, all other thoughts faded far away.

Early Wednesday morning, Desi was surprised by a text from Gunnar. Meet me at the Hjartalanda Coffee House at 11:00 a.m.

C U there, she texted back.

She rushed to finish her latest batch of calligraphy so she could mail the seventieth-birthday invitations to her long-term customer while she was in town meeting Gunnar.

Anxiety about why he wanted to see her pecked around her edges, making her fingers quiver and the letters more in line with what she imagined Elke Norling was deciphering in that pirate journal. After she'd ruined a second invitation, she gave up on the calligraphy and jumped into the shower. She'd finish the project tonight and mail the invitations tomorrow.

After wrestling into her denim leggings and a summery fuchsia smock, she skipped downstairs. "I'm going into town. You need anything?" she called out.

"I could use more of that pink stomach medicine. Got another council meeting tonight," Gerda replied from the sunroom.

Desi smiled. "You got it!" She opted to head for the door without going down the hall to say goodbye. Since she was keeping the meeting with Gunnar secret, she didn't want to lie and wasn't ready to meet her grandmother's eyes today.

Fifteen minutes later, Desi entered the coffee shop and immediately spotted Gunnar. He was talking up the waitress, who looked happy as a high schooler with a supercrush. He glanced up and waved, and Desi made her way over to his booth for two as the waitress scurried off.

He rose. "How's it going?"

"Not bad." She sat, her throat going dry. There was already water on the table, so she took a sip.

"So you're probably wondering why I asked you here."

She hoped with all of her heart it was about her father, because she really didn't want to find out Gunnar was a two-timing friend to Kent and was hitting on her behind his back. "Yes, actually."

He smiled, his intense green eyes nearly bowling

her over. "Oh, I hope you don't mind, but I ordered us both coffees already."

"That's fine."

"You want anything else? A roll or something? I like their muffins."

"I'm good. Thanks."

"Okay, so I got ahold of my guy, the P.I., the other day and fed him your information."

Returning dryness nearly shut down her throat. She couldn't swallow or respond.

Gunnar fiddled with his water glass, turning it round and round on the condensation ring on the table. The waitress was back in record time with the coffees and Gunnar's blueberry muffin. "Thanks, darlin'." He soon got sidetracked fixing his coffee and peeling the wrapper from the muffin. "Cream?" He pushed the tiny stainless-steel pitcher at her.

Desi could hardly breathe as she waited. Did he have a clue how he tortured her? She took the creamer and poured; a conspicuous tremor had her nearly missing her mug. "And?"

His gaze drifted upward from her hands to her eyes, assessing her as if she were a suspect. "And we think we got your man."

Since his text message that morning, the bubble of anxiety that had been expanding inside her chest finally burst. He'd found her father? Her ears buzzed with heady excitement, nearly making her dizzy.

"My P.I. guy came up with a couple of hits close to the same birthday, but only one turned out to be a musician. This Victor Brown is fifty years old and plays saxophone."

"Yes. That's what my mother said. He was five or

six years older than her. That could be him." So keyed up, she knew she wouldn't be able to lift her coffee mug without spilling, so she let it sit untouched.

Gunnar took an extra-large bite of his muffin, swiped the tips of his fingers and the crumbs onto the plate then dug into his shirt pocket. He handed her a folded piece of notebook paper.

Could it be that easy? Hire a P.I.—find a long-lost father? She furrowed her eyebrows and took the paper.

He must have read her doubt. "The ballpark birth date is right on target. Course, it was a big help that he's lived in the same apartment for the last thirty years. Surprising, huh?"

She carefully unfolded the paper that held the key to her other half with no hope of hiding her quivering fingers.

"I can't legally run him without cause, so I don't know if he's had priors or not, but my P.I. guy said he checks out clean on his database. For what that's worth."

"Thank you. I appreciate it." She read her father's name, address and phone number. He still lived in Portland, two and a half hours away. Her pulse went a little haywire in her chest. Would she have the nerve to call him?

"So you do whatever you want. That's up to you," he said.

She felt like a heel, but had to ask. "Could you do me a favor and not mention this to Kent?"

Gunnar's brows lowered. "After he was the one to start the ball rolling?"

"This is very personal, Gunnar." The thought of contacting her father made her tremble inside. "I don't want Kent or Gerda to know just yet." *If I fail, if my father turns out to be a bust, I want to keep it to myself. No one else could possibly understand. Especially two people who want me to stay in Heartlandia. And since I might be falling in love with one of them...*

The last thought took her breath away. Was she in love with Kent?

Gunnar shoved the last bite of his muffin into his mouth and downed the rest of the coffee, waving for the waitress to refill his cup. "I don't like it, but it's your call." With his forearms against the edge of the table, he leaned in. "In case you haven't noticed, Kent Larson is one helluva great guy."

She nodded her agreement, not needing Sergeant Norling to point it out.

"There's nothing he won't do for the people he cares about."

She kept nodding. Gunnar was preaching to the choir about Kent. But she was more than his fan; she was his lover.

"He's been kicked in the teeth by his ex-wife, and the last thing he needs is to get kicked in the teeth again by you." He leaned even closer. She'd tried to avoid his eyes, but he wouldn't let her. His index finger shot up and poked the air. "You better not hurt him." He wadded up his napkin and tossed it on the table, then sat back against the red padded booth. "That's not a threat. It's just a friend looking out for his friend." He gave her a quick, obligatory smile that disappeared instantly.

Desi wasn't about to let Gunnar rattle her any more than she already was. "I understand. But I've got to find my father, and I don't want to upset Kent for nothing. I may not even be able to reach Victor. He may not want to see me. I just need some time to figure out how to handle this, and I don't want anyone influencing me. This was between my mother and me, and I'm not even sure she wanted me to search for him. She only told me about him because she thought it was the right thing to do. That I had a right to know who my birth father was. You know?"

Desi searched Gunnar's eyes for a kernel of understanding, and thought she'd found it. "I need to go through this by myself," she whispered.

His lips made a tight line. "Like I said. He's my best friend, and I don't like to see him lied to. He's obviously crazy about you, but you've got to do what you gotta do."

As Gunnar stood, taking charge of the meeting by ending it, Desi glanced up. "Thank you. Thank you so much." She put the paper in her shoulder bag and followed him outside.

How can he know if Kent is crazy about me? And by keeping this information about my father a secret, am I lying by omission to him?

To say Gunnar made an imposing picture in his uniform didn't come close. The guy oozed authority, and Desi knew the last thing on earth she'd ever want to incur was the wrath of Sergeant Norling. But she'd come too far to abandon her plans. Finding her father had been equally important as getting to know her grandmother. She couldn't stop now. This was her life journey, and she had to walk it.

She watched from the sidewalk as Gunnar got into his squad car, nodded a goodbye and drove off. If only he could understand.

Could anyone appreciate the huge significance of finally meeting her father, besides her?

Instead of running to a quiet place and punching in the numbers on her cell phone, Desi fought off the surge of nerves throughout her body, and she was suddenly consumed with the desire to find Cliff and tell him her news. Having the support of an understanding person was good, and she didn't have to go through this entirely alone. If she needed an ally in her quest, someone to give her the courage to follow through, Cliff, a man with nothing at stake, was the one.

She hustled down three blocks to Lincoln's Place and scooted around back to the kitchen door. Thank God, he was there.

"What's up, buttercup?" Always happy to see her, Cliff welcomed her in as he stood behind a chopping board.

"I've found him."

He stopped chopping. "Your daddy?"

She nodded, digging out the paper, waving it around. "I've got his phone number and address right here. I'm so nervous I could puke."

"Not in my kitchen, sugar." He walked toward her, and she ached for his support. He wrapped his arm around her shoulders and took the paper. "Mr. Victor Brown. Mm-mm-mm." He rubbed her arm. "I'm a big jazz fan, and I've never heard of him. But that doesn't matter. When you gonna call?"

She leaned her head against Cliff's shoulder. "Would you mind if I called him from here?"

"Course not. We're friends, aren't we?"

She sighed. "Thank you." Not only was Cliff a new friend, but he was also a mentor, and besides her mother, Desi had been short on mentors throughout her twenty-eight years.

Taking the biggest leap of faith in her life, she pressed the first four digits on her cell phone. "Oh, God, I'm so nervous."

Cliff pulled her closer. "Go on, little sister. You can do it. Give your daddy a call."

She pressed the remaining digits, and then on the third ring a gravelly voice answered, "Yeah?" sounding like the phone woke him.

"Is this Victor Brown?" She flashed a fearful glance at Cliff. He gave an encouraging nod.

"Who's this?"

"My name is Desdemona Rask, the daughter of Ester Rask. Do you remember her?"

A long pause ensued, followed by shuffling of what was probably sheets and blankets, the sound of a lighter flicking, a long, slow inhalation of a cigarette and then an exhalation. "I don't know that name."

Desi's heart, so full of hope, dropped to her stomach like a lead ball. With Cliff's physical support, she stayed standing, dug deep into her well of strength and began her story. How her mother was a huge music fan. How she sneaked off to Portland several times to hear him when he played with Trevor Jones, the late, great jazz pianist. She heard Cliff acknowledge Trevor Jones's name. "Uh-huh."

But Victor kept quiet, making her wonder if he'd fallen back to sleep.

Desi continued on. She told him how Ester got pregnant, ran away from home and how she gave Desi Victor's name just before she died. "She said you were my father. That you were the only African-American man she'd ever been with."

More silence. Desi could barely breathe, his hesitation squeezed so tight around her chest.

"So what do you want from me?" he said, matter-of-factly, taking another long draw on his cigarette.

Viselike tension made it hard to form the words. "I'd like to meet you."

Chapter Eleven

That night, slowly emerging from an intense orgasm orchestrated by Kent's mouth and tongue, Desi wanted to come clean. She wanted to tell him about finding her father and the meeting she'd arranged for Friday afternoon. But she'd promised to make that journey by herself. She couldn't possibly know what the outcome might be and didn't want to upset him for nothing.

His hands bracketed her temples as he leaned on one elbow and delved deeply into her eyes. "You know what's crazy?" he said, slaying her with a dark, sexy stare.

She shook her head, still reeling from his magic, amazed by the wealth of feeling, physical and emotional, he'd gifted her. She'd never felt this way about a man before. "What?" came her barely audible reply.

His thick ridge nudged at her entrance, and she

opened her legs for him. The tip prodded her, instantly sparking renewed desire.

He edged deeper inside, his eyes still locked onto hers. She was his. His lids slipped closed in a blissful expression for a moment as they both adjusted to the physical paradise they'd come to know and share so regularly.

"You feel so damn good, Desi."

"That's not crazy. That's just good. You and me. We're good," she said, pushing her hips against him, unable to deny the truth. He was good for her, and though she wasn't sure how loving a man felt, she thought she loved him. All the more reason to finally find out who she was. Until she met her father and found out about her African-American roots, she'd always feel a part of her was missing, and how could she give Kent all of her when she wasn't yet whole?

He brushed her mouth, and she recognized her own taste on his lips. "We're damn good," he said as he moved inside her then teased and backed out a notch. Her eyelids fluttered closed as a wave of sizzling shivers raced to her core. "What's crazy is— Desi, look at me."

It took all the final threads of willpower to stop focusing on the feelings he'd set off and open her eyes and look into his heavy-lidded gaze. When she did, she saw raw desire there. That look pushed her pulse, invading it with heat that burned southward to their sex.

"Even though it's only been a couple of weeks, I've fallen for you." His eyes scanned her face in a desperate fashion. "I think about you all the time. Can't wait to hold you like this every night." He pushed deeper inside, driving her crazy, making it impossible to take in the significance of his words. "I need you."

She'd heard him correctly. He needed her. The phrase wreaked havoc with her pulse and caused her breasts to tighten and tingle. She'd never been needed before by a man. Ever.

"I'm crazy about you, too." Desi could hardly speak, she was so overcome with Kent's confession and her own deepening feelings for him.

She wrapped her thighs around his waist and they joined as close as humanly possible, rocking and jutting, changing up the rhythm until nothing but blistering desire took hold.

"I love you," he said, his mouth over her ear as he thrust deep.

She gasped. The splintering intensity from his declaration and their lovemaking nearly stole her words. He loved her, and she loved him. "I love you, too," she said on a breath, hugging his back.

Several minutes later, as he drove her over the edge to ecstasy, she hung on tight, savoring every sensation coursing and pummeling through her, holding on to Kent as if she might lose him. Never wanting to let go.

Afterward, they clung together in sweat and twisted sheets. He nuzzled and kissed her cheek. "You know what I think?"

"What?"

"That everything is pretty much perfect the way it is. You and me. Together. Steven will love having you around all the time."

"What are you saying, Kent?"

He took a slow inhalation then let it out close to her ear. "That the three of us can make our own family."

She didn't answer right away, sensing he wanted her to drop her plans, picking up on his fear of possibly losing her to a dream, like he had his ex-wife. But wasn't that exactly what she searched for—her family? She needed to find the total picture of where she'd come from, before she'd be free to be a family with Kent and Steven.

Did Kent want to marry her? Shack up? That didn't seem his style. Where exactly were they headed? If she could only figure out what she needed versus what she wanted. Right now Kent was it. He'd said the words, and she'd finally admitted out loud that she loved him back.

The frenzied questions flew through her mind. Until she could formulate her thoughts, she didn't dare broach the subject of being a family with Kent.

Giving in to exhaustion, she yawned. "I love what you're saying, baby, but let's be fair and tackle this topic when we're both rested up, okay?"

"Stay with me." It wasn't a question.

And she did, until the break of dawn, when she kissed him on the forehead and slipped across the yard to her grandmother's house.

She wanted to be everything he deserved, but until she finally found out her entire history, she'd forever be half of her whole. How could she give the man she loved half of herself when he deserved everything?

Friday afternoon, Desi sat at a table near the windows at Milo's City Cafe on Northeast Broadway in Portland, working on her second cup of coffee. It had taken over two and a half hours to get here due to city traffic, and she'd had to park at the Lloyd Center and walk over.

She'd told Gerda she wanted to spend a day shopping at the trendy mall and would be home too late for dinner. Since her uncle Erik had invited her to dinner the night before, she hadn't seen Kent since Wednesday night. When he'd told her he loved her and mentioned about them being a family. She loved Kent—God, she loved him—and Steven had stolen her heart the first day they'd met.

While Kent was at work on Thursday, she'd followed a whim and, after mailing the finished calligraphy invitations, paid another visit to the community college. Knowing a man loved her made her do crazy things. But her visit had been twofold. Gerda had spoken about Elke Norling deciphering the pirate journals, and curiosity drove Desi to get a visitor pass to sit in on one of her history courses. History of Heartlandia 101.

The young blonde bore a strong facial resemblance to Gunnar, but where Gunnar was macho and worldly, Elke dressed beyond her years, hiding a nice figure in stereotypical bookworm fashion. Where he was built like a rugby player, she was petite and fragile looking. But Elke's love of Heartlandia and the subject of the day—the influence of the Chinook native dwellers on Heartlandia's birth—caused Desi's chest to clutch.

What must it be like to be part of a place you love with all of your heart?

Desi clicked back into the here and now at the diner and checked her watch. Ten minutes to two. Victor had said he'd meet her at one. She'd ordered a piece of homemade apple pie to kill time and had only picked at the crust.

The waitress stopped by. "Don't you like it?"

"I'm just not hungry," Desi answered lamely, suspecting she'd insulted the waitress and Milo's fresh-baked-pie reputation before the middle-aged lady in standard diner uniform swept the plate away.

Hunger was the last thing on her mind, even as her stomach rumbled in protest. There was no way she could eat. Especially now, when the man purported to be her father had stood her up. Maybe he got the time wrong. Or worse, maybe he wanted nothing to do with her.

Her insides were tighter than a knotted and coiled rope. She looked around the clean, slick version of a family diner. Throughout the midcentury modern building, everyone seemed happy and deep in conversation over their food, and here she was, staring at her watch. Waiting.

To be on the safe side, Desi had only told Gunnar she'd be at the café. Guessing Gerda would tell Kent she'd gone shopping in Portland if he asked where she was, she hoped it wouldn't spark concern. After all, Kent was the person who'd started the ball rolling on finding Victor Brown. He knew Victor's last-known address was right here in Northeast Portland. Kent would put two and two together. Desi kept her fingers crossed he'd be wrapped up with work all day, followed by Friday-night pizza and video with Steven, and he wouldn't connect the dots.

She pumped her booted foot and took another sip of lukewarm coffee. How long should she wait? She speed-dialed Victor's phone. It went directly to voice mail. Great. He wasn't the least bit interested in meeting her, just like Cliff had warned.

Damn it.

She asked for a warm-up on her coffee, and just as

the waitress poured from the fresh pot, a text message came through.

Desi's pulse nearly jumped out of her chest as she read. Gig came up. Meet another day?

Devastation grabbed her by her shoulders and shook. She fisted her hands, fighting off tears.

Talk about not being interested.

How was she supposed to respond to his text? *No problem. I like to waste time. Aren't you interested in meeting your own daughter?*

Another text came through. How about Monday? Same time.

Desi paid her bill, went to the bathroom and freshened up, feeling like nothing more than an afterthought to the man, and only then begrudgingly responded, O.K.

She stepped out onto the heavily tree-lined avenue of Northeast Broadway and nearly stumbled. Another text, this one from Kent— Where are you?

In Portland.

I'm on NE Broadway. Where is Milo's City Cafe?

He was here? In Portland? She checked up and down the street, suddenly winded, as if she'd run a mile. Kent was half a block away. He strode toward her, something simmering in him.

Anxiety rippled through Desi. Gerda had given her up without a second thought, and Gunnar had probably helped Kent zero in on his mark. Why couldn't those people mind their own business?

A tiny thought planted in her brain. *Because they care about you. They told him because they care.* Victor obviously didn't give a damn, but at least he'd re-scheduled.

Desi swallowed as Kent came within hugging distance. Up close, the determined expression resembled hurt, the same emotion she was feeling from being stood up by her father.

"You didn't have any intention of letting me know why?" Kent said.

"This is between me and my father." Her knees were wobbly, but she'd stand her ground no matter how hard it was. "I didn't want to worry you, and it's important to me that I meet him."

"Worry me?" he said with a tight jaw and searching eyes.

"I didn't want to involve you because—"

"Did you even hear what I said the other night?" His voice was low and measured.

"Yes, but…"

"When I told you I loved you?"

"Yes, of course…"

"You said it back to me. Did you mean it?" His brows shot up in doubt. "Or was it just an obligatory reply?"

Could she explain how terrified she was of admitting her feelings to Kent, because it changed everything? "It's not that I don't care, because I do. Deeply. I love you, but—"

"Don't play me, Desi." His gaze delved into hers, giving her time to take in what he'd intimated, and it felt awful. "When people love each other they don't keep secrets."

"Kent, please understand."

"I'm trying, but this doesn't make a lot of sense. You

tell me you love me, we talk about getting involved, then you sneak off."

"I've been honest with you from the start. The question is, have you been listening?"

"Yes, but for me, the big question is—" his tense voice softened in tone "—do you realize what you might be running to and leaving behind?" After searching her eyes, causing her to blink, Kent scanned the area. "Where is he?"

Now she'd have to admit her defeat in front of the man she'd only just begun to love. "Didn't show." Tiny pinpricks started behind her lids.

Kent's expression softened. "I'm sorry," he said, and she believed it as he gently grasped her upper arm. "Are you ready to come home, then?"

He wanted her to give up, just like that? Did he think she was a child? She yanked her arm from his grasp and started down the street. Couldn't he understand her lifelong need to be in touch with her father's side? "We rescheduled for Monday. I've decided to stay here for the weekend."

He followed, nearly nipping at her boot heels. She knew her plans wouldn't sit well with Kent and quickened her stride until they reached an empty lot.

"Don't treat me like I'm Steven." She spun around and nailed him with all the frustration tangling her up inside.

His pained look returned. Her selfish quest had hurt Kent—the guy who wanted to protect his son from women like her—and the man did a great job of wearing his feelings on his sleeve.

But could she blame him?

She wanted to take all the anger she felt for Victor

right this moment and throw it at Kent, but he didn't deserve it. The man had been through hell and back in the past couple of years, what with his wife taking off and leaving him to raise Steven by himself. Here she was, adding to the pile.

But she couldn't back off. "If you think you can treat me like a kid because you care about me, it won't fly."

He kept his distance, dug his hands into his back pockets. "Look, I understand your need to meet this guy."

"My father," she corrected him.

"Your birth father." He took a slow breath. "I'm just asking for some honesty and consideration. That is, if you care about me at all."

She did care about him. "You know I do."

Hell, she loved him, but right now he was playing the martyr and pushing her way out of her comfort zone. She wanted to say thank-you for giving a damn and that she was sorry but she had to do what she had to do. But her tongue had gone into hiding and her throat closed. Why did everything have to be so freaking mixed-up?

He swiped fingers through his hair. "The thing is, I can't be the second choice to some guy who rescheduled. I've been through that already, and I'm no fool. Won't go there again."

She understood his angle, but he needed to give her some consideration, too. Instead he wielded a martyred sword that sliced through her heart.

Riled again, she shot back, "Are you giving me an ultimatum?"

"I'm asking you to come home with me."

She went still and spoke softly. "I need to do this my way." She needed time to herself without pressure from the people she cared about in Heartlandia trying to influence her decision.

Their gazes knotted in a standoff.

His arms went wide, palms lifted, imploring. "Damn, I knew what you planned to do all along and I still fell for you." He looked like a defeated man, his eyes drooping, shoulders hunched. "I should never have kissed you, Desi. I should have held my ground and stayed that uptight dude telling you to stay away from my son." There was pleading and love in his eyes. "But I couldn't resist you and took it a helluva lot further than kissing." He approached, played with the curls of hair around her shoulders as if he'd never seen or touched them before. "I walked right into your beauty and charms and fell for you, and now I feel like a fool."

He'd taken a knife to her core and sliced right through, pain penetrating every nerve. She'd hurt him, the only man who'd ever really cared about her. She shook her head, her blurred vision making him into a melting hero. She could barely utter *sorry*.

"You're not a fool," she managed to get out.

"Then what am I? You tell me."

"You're a good man who I've been lucky enough to meet." One thing was clear—she didn't deserve him, not when she'd already hurt him and all he wanted was the best for her.

Kent straightened, pulling himself together. His eyes flashed with thoughts, his jaw twitched, biting them back, but he wouldn't stop. "You don't need some stranger to tell you who you are. You need to look inside to find that out. If that's not enough, look to Gerda, to your uncle and aunt, to Heartlandia." He gave a wan smile. "Here's a good one—look to Steven and me. You want to find out who you are then we've all got the answers. You don't need this guy who doesn't show up. Who hasn't ever shown up."

"Stop it. Just stop right there. Don't tell me how to think or what to say. This is my issue and we aren't going to solve it on your terms. Can't you try to understand what this means to me?"

He pinched the bridge of his nose, as if his head was ready to explode. "I'm trying, Desi. I'm trying, but I just don't get it."

"No, you're not trying. You're trying to bulldoze me into doing things your way." She glanced at him as the hint of chagrin changed his stern expression. "You don't have to get it. Just let me work things out on my own terms. Can you do that?"

More mixed-up than ever whether this was the right thing to do or not—was Victor Brown worth it?—she stood determined. There was no going back on this quest.

"Come home with me." His words were quiet and controlled as he tested her.

She dug in her heels and, full of fear and misgivings, went for it. "Please, Kent. Give me some time to discover the rest of myself." She touched his arm, engaging his stressed and weary eyes. "I do love you—please know that. And I'm not like your ex-wife." She'd played dirty, struck a chord, and his gaze faltered. "I need this. I need to meet my father." She touched his other arm and squeezed both. "That's all I'm asking, and I need you to understand that."

They shared a silent deadlock. She thought of another angle to get through to him. "If you love me, you have to trust me. Let me stay here, see this out."

His jaw tensed and his Adam's apple bobbed in a slow, silent swallow. "How long?"

Maybe she'd gotten through to him. Maybe he finally understood how this meeting went to the root of her whole being. "Until I finally know for sure who I am. Until I find out about all of me."

That could take forever. Kent shook his head in defeat. Every sinew and cell in his body ached. He'd lost her, and he'd only just fallen for her. She asked for the one thing he wasn't prepared to give. Trust. Not yet, anyway.

She'd asked him to trust her. It seemed just out of his reach, beyond any capability to ever trust a woman again. Diana had made sure of that. She'd started out the same way, little fun visits to San Francisco, soon needing her S.F. fix at least once a month, then she moved on to her monthly girls' week of shopping there. Hell, she'd even planned a week's vacation in San Francisco when she knew Kent couldn't get away from the Urgent Care. Then she dropped the bomb about them moving. Turned out she'd been seeing a real-estate agent, looking for the perfect house. Had plans to put Steven in boarding school. And when he said no, she left and never came back. Now she worked for that guy and probably lived with him, too.

If he left Desi in Portland, it might be the beginning to her never coming back. Her seeking her past could make history repeat itself for him. Talk about lousy timing. He wanted to kick himself for letting down his guard and falling in love with her. He wanted to cuss every foul word he'd ever learned. He'd known better from the start, yet, because he didn't have a clue how to do casual, he'd let it happen, fallen in love, head over heels. Like a complete fool.

He did love her, which was why right now, this instant, he had to prove it to her by taking the hardest test of his life. He had to take her at her word, risk trusting her, once again trusting a woman he loved. Would it end up the way it had with Diana, or was this the only way to prove to Desi he wasn't just saying words when he'd said "I love you"?

"I'm just two and a half hours away. It's not like I'm halfway around the world," she said.

"The way I feel right now, you may as well be."

"I won't shut you out, Kent. I promise."

She said she needed this. He saw the driven expression in her eyes pleading for his understanding. He had to believe how important this was for her. He studied her, saw a woman with tortured determination written all over her beautiful face. She wouldn't back down, and there was something else he noticed—she needed his trust as much as she needed this Victor person to show up.

If he loved her, he couldn't demand her to come home with him like he wanted with every fiber in his body. He had to be bigger than his insecurity.

He rubbed his beard. "Okay. We'll do it your way." It came out gruffer than he'd meant, but her expression brightened anyway.

"I promise, no matter what, I'll be back in Heartlandia by Monday night." Her beautiful mahogany eyes danced while she spoke.

Kent had to believe her. He couldn't let his worst fears take hold. Not right now. Yet the thought of losing

Desi gripped his core and nearly squeezed the breath out of him.

He loved her and wanted the best for her, and in his mind that meant her being with him...yet her eyes shone through the disappointment today.

She'd told him right from the start she was looking for her father. There was no guessing what might happen until she actually met him. This meeting might mean getting to know a whole different family and spending time with them, and that could change everything.

But she needed him to be on her side. The least he could do was give her hope, something he felt slipping through his grasp. Her father better not stand her up again or Kent would find him and deliver his message personally.

Because he loved her, he forced his fingers to relax and nodded, doing the toughest thing he'd ever had to do: pretend he could deal with this and trust she'd still want him. "Okay. Good luck. See you Monday."

Kent kissed Desi lightly, barely holding himself together, and turned to leave.

She'd promised to come back to Heartlandia, but when she did, depending on what went down with her father, it might be only the first step toward saying goodbye.

Chapter Twelve

Desi spent the weekend at an inexpensive motel, using the one and only credit card she kept for emergencies. She'd paid off her mother's medical bills by selling the house, had been living on the grace of her grandmother and until now had been able to meet her personal expenses with her calligraphy money and posing for the art class. She could count on being paid soon for the invitations she'd finished and mailed before leaving for Portland, which would help pay for the motel.

She'd called her grandmother Friday night, after she'd calmed down from her encounter with Kent. Then she told a little white lie about loving the city and wanting to stick around for the weekend, see more of the sights. Mostly, she stayed in her room and thought.

Thinking about Kent roiled up so many emotions that she didn't know what to do. Thoughts of her grandmother made her wish they'd devoured all of those boxes of pictures and mementos about her mother. Somehow, they'd never gotten back to walking memory lane after Gerda's medical episode and escalating mayoral duties.

As she anticipated her meeting with her father later that afternoon, jitters set in. A million questions whirled around her head. Would he even show up?

She held a hopeful fantasy that he'd greet her with the same open arms her grandma had, invite her into his life and share his relatives—her relatives—with her. Maybe he'd ask her to go on the road with him some-time, not that she would. She'd had enough of that with her mother while growing up, but being asked would be nice. Finally, she'd learn about her African-American heritage. Be a part of it. Own it. Know who she was and where she'd come from. Finally, she'd come face-to-face with her other half. If he did open up to her, she couldn't just walk away from the offer.

That was what Kent must have picked up on before—her desperate need to discover her living family and learn the culture. To finally become two halves of a whole. To understand why, no matter how much she loved her mother, she'd always felt different from her. She needed to face her other half and embrace it, and Kent somehow sensed that would take her away.

If he loved her, wouldn't he want that for her? Or was she being totally selfish?

And if she was being selfish, would he wait for her to come back? The thought of losing him sent a shudder through her.

She packed the few items she'd brought with her to Portland after putting on the same jeans and boots she'd worn for the past three days. Saturday, she'd crossed the Willamette River and gone to the Portland Art Museum. Yesterday, she'd found a flea market in the North-east Broadway neighborhood and splurged on a new top. The zebra-patterned top had a drawstring neckline and loose, three-quarter sleeves. She'd found a clunky handmade necklace made out of huge green and tur-quoise buttons, with a matching bracelet to add some color. All at a great price. She parted her hair down the middle and let it go curlier than usual. How was a girl supposed to dress to meet her father for the first time in twenty-eight years?

After she checked out from the motor lodge, she drove back to Northeast Broadway and began her search for a parking spot, then wandered the trendy area on foot until it was time to meet her dad. Could she call him Dad? Wasn't that something a person would call a man they knew instead of a stranger? Maybe after today…

Milo's was packed with the lunch crowd at twelve forty-five. She put in her name for a table and waited outside on a bench with several other people. The day was clear and warm, and she closed her eyes to let the sun calm her.

Late last night she'd made her peace with the proba-bility that this meeting, if it actually occurred, would be awkward and most likely disappointing. Just like Cliff had warned. She'd also decided that if Victor Brown didn't show up today, she'd let it be and not try to con-tact him again. She wasn't dense. If he didn't come today, she'd know he didn't give a rip about her. Yet she still held out hope.

"Desi?" a gravelly voice said near her.

Her eyes flew open to find a tall, thin man in jeans and a black leather jacket and gray T-shirt with Montreux

Jazz Festival 2010 splashed across his narrow chest. What did she expect—a dashiki with a kufi cap? Victor Brown stood in front of her, and she finally knew from whom she'd gotten her freckles. The man's dark bronze face was splattered with them.

"Yes. Hi," she said, fighting off the rush of tingling nerves and standing to shake his hand.

He bypassed her hand and gave her a friendly hug. He smelled of tobacco and biting cologne. He didn't hold her long, and the hug wasn't really affectionate or inviting, but more like a professional guy who knew how to greet people to make them feel welcomed. A smooth operator.

"I'm Vic. Let me have a look at you." His birth date made him fifty, and the roadmap of wrinkles on his face bore that out. Those nearly black eyes were friendly and warm. His wide smile revealed smoker's teeth. Tight black hair was kept short and clean-cut with silver strands here and there. He had a soul patch but no other facial hair, expensive-looking diamond studs in both ears and wore several huge rings on both hands. "Damn, you're a looker." He laughed and it turned into a cough.

After warding off an icky feeling from her birth father's first reaction to her, she forced a smile. "Thanks."

A moment or two of awkward silence followed. "So how you been?" he asked, all upbeat. "That's lame, isn't it? I should say, where do we begin?" His voice reminded her of the actor Samuel L. Jackson.

"I know," she said. "How *do* we start?"

The waitress saved them another uneasy moment by calling Desi's name for a table. Suddenly all business, they followed her inside and found their spot, quickly ordering coffee and focusing on the menu instead of each other.

Desi thought of ten different ways to start a conversation, but Victor beat her to the punch. "You live around here?"

"No. My mother and I last lived in the Los Angeles area." She zeroed in on him. "Do you remember my mother yet?"

His glance skipped around like a man put on the spot. Desi dug into her purse for a photo that Gerda had given her, the high school senior picture. She showed it to him, figuring it would make the most sense, being the one closest to when he'd known her. He took it and studied, and Desi watched as she imagined he recognized Ester and maybe flashed through some special memories.

But he shook his head slowly. "She's beautiful, and you'd think I'd remember a woman like that, but…"

Desi took back the picture, awash in disappointment. "It was a long time ago." How many gorgeous blondes had the guy been with? "About twenty-nine years." She waited for him to look at her. "I'm twenty-eight."

He rubbed his face, a hint of regret in his eyes. "Look, I've traveled around the world half a dozen times. I'm in different clubs every other week when I work. I get on airplanes and show up in cities in time for the gigs, play all night, sleep all day, then move on to the next job. Most of my life is a blur. You know what I'm sayin'?"

She could understand his point. Hell, maybe there were hundreds of Desis around the globe, too.

"My mother met you when you were playing with Trevor Jones right here in Portland."

He made an exaggerated nod. "Mmm. Yes. I worked

with him for a couple of years. Best money I ever made until he died in that car crash."

The waitress showed up and took their orders, giving Desi time to regroup from the letdown. *Remember, Cliff told you to expect this.*

"Mom was a pretty young blonde who loved music."

"Mmm, known a few of those, too." He evaded her eyes, pouring two packets of sugar into his coffee, started to stir then stopped. "Look, I don't mean to disappoint you, but even though your mother is a gorgeous woman and all, I don't—"

"Was."

He looked up, a question in his eyes.

"She died last year. She'd played piano in so many hotels and bars over the years, the best I can figure is she got lung cancer from secondhand smoke, because she never smoked."

"Your momma was a musician?"

"Ester Rask was known throughout the Midwest as one of the best hotel and piano-bar musicians in the country." The old, familiar pride welled up in Desi's chest as she talked about her mother, whom she loved with all of her heart, and her mother's talent. She'd had a worldwide and centuries-old songbook memorized right inside her head. Throw her a title and she'd play it with practiced perfection. "But she never caught her break. You know?"

"Tell me about it. I've scraped by barely making a living most of my life, playing sax in the background of all the greats. I'll be fifty-one this November and I'm working as hard now as when I was twenty-five."

The waitress delivered their omelets and Victor salted his heavily. "There's no money in this field unless you hit it big. I'm just a backup man." He reached for the ketchup. "Don't get me wrong, I love what I do. I just make enough for me. That's all."

He squinted one eye and trained his gaze squarely on her. "So if this is about money..."

Anger flashed through Desi. She bit back the first words she thought and the curses. No need to insult the man. "Not what I'm after."

Things went quiet and tension counted out the next minute or two as they both dived into their food. He ate with gusto, a free bird in the world of responsibilities. She mostly moved her potatoes and eggs around the plate.

"Are you married?" She wasn't ready to give up yet.

Victor pushed out his bottom lip and shook his head. "No, ma'am. Not my style. The world is my home and whatever band I'm working with, my family."

She was beginning to see a pattern here. No strings. No commitments. Just his saxophone, music and the road. He probably had women he hooked up with in every city he worked—his regulars. She stopped her bitter thoughts before they could eat away at her and ruin what little of her appetite was left. *Keep it light. Find out what you can.* Wasn't that her plan? "Do you have family here in Oregon?"

"Nah. Mom and Dad are both dead. I've got a brother somewhere back in North Carolina. Haven't seen him in years. My sister lives in Colorado. Sometimes I go to Denver for Christmas, when I'm in the country."

Truth was, his lifestyle seemed a little sad and very lonely.

"Do you have any pictures of your brother and sister?" *My aunt and uncle?* "And their kids?" *My cousins.*

He screwed up his face. "Nah. I know what they look like. Least I used to." He kept shoving food into his mouth, eating as if there were no tomorrow.

"How about your mom and dad—what did they do?"

"The old man sold cars, and my momma was a bookkeeper. We got by okay." Now he started on his toast and slathered it with blackberry jam nearly half an inch thick. He'd stopped talking, obviously having no intention of sharing anything about his heritage.

She was searching for her history and he just didn't get it. Every answer revolved around him and what he did or thought. When it came to talking about his roots, he got tight-lipped. The fact that he had no clue what she needed gave her pause.

Desi abandoned that line of questioning and diverted the conversation to things Victor could brag about by asking about all the musicians he'd worked with. Pride shone through his face, and she heard it in his voice as he ran down the long list of music-related accomplishments.

She had to admit he'd played with some greats, and she was impressed with his solid star-power credentials. But now what? The man hadn't asked one question about her personally.

"Sorry I had to stand you up the other day," he said. "I take studio jobs whenever I can get them, and a commercial jingle came up." He nailed her with his penetrating dark eyes. "That's the name of the game. You pick up work, make money when you can. Can't always get another gig lined up before you finish another." He used his butter knife like a pointer stick. "I go through dry spells and have to live off what little savings I have. So, again, if this is about money…"

She let out an exasperated sigh. "I told you, I'm not after anything. I just hoped to find out about my African-American roots."

He laughed. It turned into another phlegmy cough. "Well, from what I learned in school, we came over in boats." He noticed how badly that comment had gone over. "My people moved out west from Mississippi back in the fifties. That's all I've got for you." He pushed his chair back from the table. "I need a cigarette. Be right back."

Desi watched his cool stroll toward the door. He was what he was, and there wasn't anything much he cared to share with her. She lost the last inkling of her appetite and put down her fork.

All her life she'd heard the phrase *blood is thicker than water* and took it to mean the bonds between relatives were closer, stronger than friends. She imagined how it would be to have a big family. Longed for it. She took a sip of water. The saying seemed upside down to her. Sure, the bond she and her mother had was broken only by death. But looking at the man outside sucking smoke into his lungs, the one who couldn't even remember doing the deed the night Desi was conceived, she felt…well…nothing. Absolutely nothing. Yet some of his blood ran through her veins.

Desi thought about her grandma Gerda. It was a whole different story. Relatives needed to *want* to be close, not stay connected just because they shared the same DNA. In Victor's case, their DNA meant squat. He was a complete stranger. Why would he want anything to do with a daughter at this late stage in his life? So far he hadn't offered one reason to pursue one another, and she couldn't really blame him, not with the life he led.

Now he was on his cell phone, and it reminded her about the text message Kent had sent that morning. I hope you find what you're looking for then come back to me.

It had made her cry then and thinking about it almost started her up again now. All she could think to say in return was *I hope I do, too*. Talk about noncommittal. Hell, she could give Victor Brown a run for his money on that one. Quickly dabbing the corners of her eyes, she hoped Victor wouldn't notice now that he was heading back inside.

Nah, that saying about blood and water was all sideways. Love was thicker than blood, and just because she shared the man's DNA didn't make him family. Hell, Cliff was closer to her than the man sitting back down across the table.

Kent's handsome face came to mind again, the man she'd fallen in love with. She made a rueful smile. Then, knowing that he loved and waited for her, the smile changed into a grin straight from her heart.

"What you so happy about?" Victor asked.

"I'm just thinking about my friends."

"That's all we've got, you know?" He sat sideways on his chair, going philosophical on her.

She nodded in agreement. He reached into his wallet, pulled out some cash. She reached for her purse.

"Let me get this," he said. "It's the least I can do." He smiled at her with his Morgan Freeman complexion and gentle eyes. "I do remember your momma. I had a cigarette and did some thinking. I remember. But it wasn't like we really knew each other or anything. You know what I mean?"

Feeling a blush come on—yes, she got the one-night stand part—Desi smiled awkwardly. "I get it. Thanks."

"If it's any consolation, I did try to look her up again, but it was like she'd disappeared."

Well, she had.

"Here's my card," he said, sliding all the information she'd probably ever know about Victor Brown across the table. "I'm leaving for a month in Japan this Friday, but maybe when I get back we can talk again."

"That would be nice. Thank you. Oh, and here's my card. Well, it's my business card for the small calligraphy side jobs I do."

He took it, looking less than impressed.

"I play the piano, too. Like my mother. In fact, I'm thinking of taking a job playing in a restaurant where I'm living now."

"That's good. Real good. Maybe I'll come out and hear you sometime."

"Sure."

She realized she didn't want to share Heartlandia with Victor. Not yet, anyway. Maybe when he got back from Japan she'd give him a call if he didn't call her. Give him one more chance to reach out to her. If he didn't, she'd cut her losses.

She stood and he joined her, the distance between them growing wider by the second. He had things to do and places to go. Thank God, so did she.

After Victor kissed her cheek, making her nose twitch with his potent cologne, and they said their tepid goodbyes, she walked back to her car. It would be a long drive home and she'd need the time to digest everything that had happened.

Home.

She thought about Heartlandia with the silly town slogan: Find Your Home in Heartlandia. It didn't seem quite so silly now, though; it suddenly had taken on a whole new meaning. It was a place where she could see herself putting down roots. Her own roots.

Her steps sped up into a jog as she thought about Kent.

Had she blown it with the man she loved? She prayed she hadn't broken his heart by refusing to go back with him Friday, though if he loved her the way he'd said, she probably had.

Maybe he'd finally understand her hell-bent need to face her father once she told him the whole story. From now on, if he'd still have her, she'd tell him everything. Everything.

She ran the last half block to her parked car and stumbled with one worrisome thought.

Would Kent forgive her?

There was only one way to find out. She had to go back and face him on his own turf and somehow make him know that her wandering days were over, because she'd found her family. Grandma. How could she begin to thank her for taking her in unconditionally? Kent. She sighed with the rush of memories connected to him like life and breath itself. And Steven, a little boy who missed and needed a mother figure…like a most excellent piano teacher.

She smiled to herself. Love *was* thicker than blood. Hands down.

After unlocking the car, she slid inside and sat straight. She'd met her other half and finally discovered something she'd kept hidden inside. Kind of like Dorothy in

The Wizard of Oz, turned out she'd known who she was all along. Just like Kent and Cliff had been telling her.

She was Ester Rask's kid from a hot one-night stand with Victor Brown, and Gerda and Edvard Rask's granddaughter. She was every state and city she'd ever traveled through, every book she'd ever read and every crazy job she'd ever taken.

She was a homeschooled girl, a woman with potential, and what she wanted more than anything else on the earth right at this given moment was a home…with a ready-made family. Steven. And Kent. *Please take me back.*

She pulled out of the parking lot, pushed that 1992 gas pedal to the metal and put those treads to the road. Maybe she could beat the time it took to get to Portland on the way back.

Even if Kent didn't want her back today, she'd be prepared to stick around in Heartlandia until she could convince him that she was the best thing in the world for him. That she'd never leave again without him or his blessing. She'd strut around in sexy clothes and make the man drool until he caved and made love to her again.

Grinning wide, she put in her ear pods, and knowing Kent was at work, she speed-dialed Cliff to tell him the whole story about her long-lost father.

If she timed it right, she'd make it home before the administration office at the city college closed. She'd stop there first since Gerda would be at city hall.

Good thing she'd kept all of her options open before she'd left town on Friday.

Desi parked the car in the garage right before five that afternoon. She rushed inside the house to tell her grandmother how much she loved her and to get cleaned up before Kent came home from work.

Gerda wasn't home. Obviously she was still working at city hall today like every other Monday. She wandered to the kitchen and found a note on the island and next to it an empty medicine cup with dried antacid inside. Desi picked up the note, first glancing around the grand old kitchen she'd come to love, the heart of the house where she and Gerda met up each and every morning. She was glad to be home. So, so glad.

"I have some important town business to tend to. Don't wait up for me. Love, G."

Overwhelmed with fondness for her grandmother, Desi smiled as her eyes brimmed with tears. She picked up the empty medicine cup, worrying it might not be enough to deal with the burden of being a mayor with a big town secret and wondering what more they might find out about their pirate problem tonight.

She dashed upstairs and showered, then put on the colorful sundress she knew Kent liked, judging by the way he'd quickly ripped it off her one night last week. He usually got home around sixish on Mondays, but with his busy clinic she couldn't count on it. She took time to put on makeup and the sparkly pink lipstick Kent liked to stare at whenever she wore it…right before he'd kiss it off her.

There were a million things she wanted to share with Kent, but how should she approach him? She went outside and sat on the front porch on her favorite wicker seat with the purple-paisley-patterned pillow, needing time to gather her thoughts. Way off in the distance, over the homes, buildings and train station down by the docks, and under the long arching bridge to Washington, she glimpsed a section of sparkling teal-colored Columbia River. She'd never get tired of the view.

A bicycle whizzed by on the sidewalk, shaking her out of her thoughts. It was Steven, riding like the wind on his two-wheeler to God knew where. Her tummy jumped. Noticing her, he hit his brake and laid a skid mark on the sidewalk.

"Cool. Did you see that?" he asked, as if nothing had changed.

"That was something, all right. You planning on becoming a stunt man?"

"Nah. I'm gonna be a marine biologist and a famous musician. Where've you been?"

The kid always slayed her with his innocent wit. "I've been looking for my father."

"Why'd you want to do that?"

Desi shrugged.

"Steven!" From the front door, Kent's voice cut through her peace. Adrenaline fired scattershot inside her chest. He must have gotten home while she was showering.

"Coming. Desi's home!" Steven threw his leg over the bicycle seat and prepared to head back. "See ya," he said with certainty.

Desi stood even as her stomach dropped to what seemed like her toes. She hadn't a clue how to say everything she needed to tell Kent. He saw her and stepped outside, walking her way with assured steps. She fought off the urge to run and jump into his arms, and by his slowing pace, she figured she'd made the right decision in holding back. The man must need some extra time to work out all his thoughts and what he planned to say. Just like she did.

They were within three feet of each other. His cautious expression masked the handsome curves and angles of his face.

She couldn't hold her thoughts inside another second. "I love you," she blurted, diving point-blank into the heart of everything.

Those blue-as-the-Columbia-River eyes reacted to her words by widening almost imperceptibly. His mouth followed with a twitch at the corner.

"Can you forgive me for putting you through this?" She'd hit her stride now, her long list of things to tell him working their way out of her mouth through a tunnel from her heart. "Will you please trust me now when I say I intend to stay in Heartlandia?"

They were arm's length apart. She lifted her hands for him to take, but instead his hands came from beneath and merely touched the tips of her fingers as if testing if she were real. She wanted to grab him and never let go, but she understood his hesitation. She'd hurt him. Deeply.

"Did he show?"

She nodded.

"And…"

"It was okay. I'll tell you about it sometime. So do you trust me now?"

"If I trust you this time, what insurance do I have you won't leave again, later?"

Normally, she loved it when he played hard to get, but right now it irritated her. "You want proof?"

"Damn right I do." His hands had come to rest on his hips, like a pouting Nordic god.

She'd take that challenge.

"I'll be right back." Desi rushed up the walkway and the steps and into the house, knowing Kent watched her every move. "Don't move." She'd also noticed his immediate reaction to the dress when his gaze had started at her shoulders and followed all the way down to her sandaled feet. *Good call on the dress!*

"Did you get a note from your father or something?" he called out in an acerbic tone.

Just before she went inside the house, she made an exaggerated and playful turn. "Nice one, Larson. You been taking comedy lessons from Steven?"

He bit his lower lip rather than smile, then stared at her long and hard, waiting.

As she ran up the stairs to her bedroom, she marveled how his words would have hurt her if he'd said them before she'd gone to Portland, but right now his comment rolled off her back.

She'd finally figured out that she was good enough just the way she was. That she was exactly what he needed. She'd also learned who she was, imperfections and all, and who she loved and where she belonged and what she wanted to be and who she wanted to be with. And because of all those things, she could understand his hurt and anger about her leaving. His cutting remark just now came from being hurt, plain and simple. She'd walked away from him, and he'd been wiser than her, knowing everything she could possibly want or need had been right under her nose. Yet she couldn't see it. Not then.

She shuffled through the piles of papers on her desk. If she played her cards right, she and Kent would have plenty of tiffs down the road, because wasn't that part of being a couple? Working things out? She grinned. Making up would always be the fun part.

There it was. She'd thrown the printout on the desk

last Thursday, and when she'd paid today they'd given her a receipt, which she'd stapled to it. She grabbed the paper and her cell phone. She'd promised Cliff a final answer by the end of happy hour today.

Stepping outside, cell phone to her ear, she saw the look of confusion on Kent's face as she walked toward him. His brows shot together and the corner of his mouth hitched high. It made her smile even wider, and she approached Kent with the confidence of a model walking the runway. She held up a finger when Kent started to ask a question. One moment, she indicated. *Keep him waiting, but not for long.*

"Hello, Cliff? Hey, it's Desi. Okay, I'm in. I'm going to take the job at your restaurant."

"So li'l bit finally came to her senses," Cliff said in his droll manner.

"For the record, I expect to work for more than just tips."

"You got it. See you this Friday."

"See you then." She shut down her cell phone and dropped it into the large pocket on her full skirt. "See?" she said, engaging and holding Kent's gorgeous stare. "I just took that job. Can't very well go traipsing off here and there and hold down a job, too, can I?"

He stepped closer, looking much more convinced with a simmering expression taking hold and promising to soon change to smoldering. "No, you can't."

In her other hand, between her thumb and index finger, she flapped the paper printout in the air. "And I have more proof."

Now looking more relaxed by the instant, Kent played along. Without saying a word, he gestured with his fingers for her to come closer. His wish was her command. She stepped forward and tossed the paper at him.

"That's my enrollment form for twelve units at Heartlandia City College for the fall semester." He caught it with the finesse of a highly paid athlete. "I'll be majoring in art design with a minor in African-American studies. How about that?"

Kent took one glance at the list of classes and dropped the paper in order to take her into his arms. They hugged as if they hadn't seen each other in a year. Damn, he felt great. She wanted to tell him how excited she was to finally start college, but his incoming kiss stole her words.

I rest my case.

His mouth felt like a little piece of heaven on her lips. She went up on tiptoes and folded her arms around his shoulders, her hands caressing his neck. After a long and thorough welcome home, he pulled away.

"Now you'll be the one painting those nude models in the Life Art class, instead of modeling for them."

She nipped his chin and caught the corner of his mouth with a quick kiss, then, for the benefit of Steven being within earshot, she whispered into the shell of Kent's ear, "From now on, the only nude modeling I'll do is for you."

That got the exact reaction she'd hoped for. His second wave of kisses traced across her jaw and cheek, soon centering on her mouth again. She angled her head in a new direction to better capture his lips. His tongue had already shifted to *come play with me* mode.

"Wow, twelve whole units," Steven said nearby, having retrieved the paper and examined it. "What are 'units'?"

Laughter cut their escalating make-out session short.

Steven stood there waving the paper around, a perplexed look on his face.

"'Units' are what each class in college counts as. Twelve units equal four classes," Desi said. She held back on her need to explain to Kent that she'd decided to start at a reasonable pace and maybe take more classes in her second semester. Surely he'd understand.

"Does this mean you'll have lots of homework like me?"

Desi's eyes stayed trained on the man she loved as she answered Steven. "Yes, I'm going to have lots and lots of homework." She kissed Kent again, but only quickly. When she pulled back, his intense gaze let her know there would also be lots of making up to do for their lost weekend.

Warmth fanned out across her body, a response she'd have to get used to, being around Kent Larson day in and day out.

Steven grabbed her hand and then his father's. "Do you guys have to kiss so much? That's gross."

"Get used to it," Kent said as they walked together toward his house. "Stay for dinner with us?" He squeezed her hand.

"Love to. Gerda's running a council meeting. Won't be home until late." By the quick, satisfied glance he gave, he'd picked up on her hidden meaning. She offered her version of a Mona Lisa smile.

As Kent headed off toward the kitchen, and Steven ran for the keyboard, she followed the boy and helped him with his music lesson.

From the kitchen, she heard Kent call out, "Sandwiches okay?"

"Yes!" Steven said, as if having a sandwich for dinner was an extra-special treat.

"Fine with me," she chimed in. Who cared what he served? Everything tasted great when you were in love anyway.

Kent continued to bang around in the kitchen, and Steven showed Desi how he'd embellished his latest piano piece with some fancy finger work.

She took it all in, marveling how everything felt just right. Couldn't be more perfect.

Just like she'd always dreamed her first real home with her newfound family would be.

* * * * *

REQUEST YOUR FREE BOOKS!

2 FREE NOVELS PLUS 2 FREE GIFTS!

⟨H⟩ HARLEQUIN®

SPECIAL EDITION

Life, Love & Family

YES! Please send me 2 FREE Harlequin® Special Edition novels and my 2 FREE gifts (gifts are worth about $10). After receiving them, if I don't wish to receive any more books, I can return the shipping statement marked "cancel." If I don't cancel, I will receive 6 brand-new novels every month and be billed just $4.74 per book in the U.S. or $5.24 per book in Canada. That's a savings of at least 14% off the cover price! It's quite a bargain! Shipping and handling is just 50¢ per book in the U.S. and 75¢ per book in Canada.* I understand that accepting the 2 free books and gifts places me under no obligation to buy anything. I can always return a shipment and cancel at any time. Even if I never buy another book, the two free books and gifts are mine to keep forever.

235/335 HDN F45Y

Name	(PLEASE PRINT)

Address	Apt. #

City	State/Prov.	Zip/Postal Code

Signature (if under 18, a parent or guardian must sign)

Mail to the Harlequin® Reader Service:
IN U.S.A.: P.O. Box 1867, Buffalo, NY 14240-1867
IN CANADA: P.O. Box 609, Fort Erie, Ontario L2A 5X3

Want to try two free books from another line?
Call 1-800-873-8635 or visit www.ReaderService.com.

* Terms and prices subject to change without notice. Prices do not include applicable taxes. Sales tax applicable in N.Y. Canadian residents will be charged applicable taxes. Offer not valid in Quebec. This offer is limited to one order per household. Not valid for current subscribers to Harlequin Special Edition books. All orders subject to credit approval. Credit or debit balances in a customer's account(s) may be offset by any other outstanding balance owed by or to the customer. Please allow 4 to 6 weeks for delivery. Offer available while quantities last.

Your Privacy—The Harlequin® Reader Service is committed to protecting your privacy. Our Privacy Policy is available online at www.ReaderService.com or upon request from the Harlequin Reader Service.

We make a portion of our mailing list available to reputable third parties that offer products we believe may interest you. If you prefer that we not exchange your name with third parties, or if you wish to clarify or modify your communication preferences, please visit us at www.ReaderService.com/consumerschoice or write to us at Harlequin Reader Service Preference Service, P.O. Box 9062, Buffalo, NY 14269. Include your complete name and address.

HSE13R

Looking to create his own legacy, Daniel Garrett wanted out of the family business. But the only way to gain access to his trust fund was to get married. So he convinced his best friend, Kenna Scott, to play the role of blushing bride. What could go wrong when they sealed their "vows" with a kiss that set off sparks?

***

"You set out the terms," she reminded him. "A one-year marriage on paper only."

"What if I want to renegotiate?" he asked.

Kenna shook her head. "Not going to happen."

"You know I can't resist a challenge."

Her gaze dropped to the towel slung around his waist and her breath hitched.

She moistened her lips with the tip of her tongue, drawing his attention to the tempting curve of her mouth. And he was tempted.

One simple kiss had blown the boundaries of his relationship with Kenna to smithereens and he didn't know how to reestablish them. Or even if he wanted to.

"Aren't you the least bit curious about how it might be between us?"

"No," she said, though her inability to meet his gaze made him suspect it was a lie. "I'd prefer to maintain my unique status as one of only a handful of women in Charisma who haven't slept with you."

"I haven't slept with half as many women as you think," he told her. "And I know what you're doing."

"What?"

"Deflecting. Trying to annoy me so that I stop wondering what you're wearing under that dress."

She shook her head, but the hint of a smile tugged at the corners of her mouth. "There's French toast and bacon in the oven, if you want it."

"I want to know if you really wear that stuff."

"No, I just buy it to take up storage space and torture your imagination."

"You're a cruel woman, Mrs. Garrett."

She tossed a saucy smile over her shoulder. "Have a good day, Mr. Garrett."

When Kenna left, he poured himself a mug of coffee and sat down with the hot breakfast she'd left for him.

He had a feeling the coming year was going to be the longest twelve months of his life.

***

Don't miss
A WIFE FOR ONE YEAR *by award-winning author*
Brenda Harlen, the next book in her new
Harlequin® Special Edition miniseries
THOSE ENGAGING GARRETTS!
On sale August 2014,
wherever Harlequin books are sold.

SPECIAL EDITION

Life, Love and Family

Coming in August 2014

ONE TALL, DUSTY COWBOY
by *USA TODAY* bestselling author
Stella Bagwell

Nurse Lilly Lockett is on a mission—to heal the patriarch of the Calhoun ranching clan. There, she meets the irresistibly rakish Rafe Calhoun, the ranch's foreman. Love has burned Lilly in the past, but the remedy for her heartbreak might just lie in the freewheeling bachelor she's tried so hard to resist!

Don't miss the latest edition of the
***Men of the West* miniseries!**

Look for THE BABY TRUTH,
already available from the
MEN OF THE WEST *miniseries by Stella Bagwell!*

Available wherever books and ebooks are sold!

www.Harlequin.com

HSE65831